WINDSTONE

MIKE MITCHELL

NEW FORUM BOOKS

FIRST NEW FORUM EDITION

Copyright © 2017 Michael Mitchell

ALL RIGHTS RESERVED

The characters in this book are entirely imaginary and bear no relation whatsoever to any living person.

Front cover art by the author

ISBN – eBook: 978-0-9995797-0-1
ISBN – Printed Edition: 978-0-9995797-1-8

Printed in the United States of America

To Rachel McAdams & Frances Sternhagen
for the initial inspiration

to Joanne Minutello, Marcus Lazzaro and Mary O'Rourke for their unwavering support of this project

and to the memory of
Margaret LaFarge Osborn and Rose Hopkins

To Kim
all the best

AUTHOR'S NOTE

This novel (or, to be precise, about half of this novel) owes its existence to a screenplay I recently wrote—which, in turn, will owe its final draft to this novel.

Although I had originally conceived the story for two of my favorite actresses, who also happen to be friends of mine, I had the feeling, almost from the outset, that the story was intended to make its debut as a novel—and I'm pleased to say that, from the day I wrote the very first page of this book, every page that followed has reinforced my conviction that this was the appropriate process for this story.

Thanks are owed to many friends and colleagues, particularly Pamela Blackwell, Laura Kay Coggeshall, Joel Edwards, Betty Etheredge, Jeanne Montano Giannetta, Harry McNally, Hugh Ross, Dana Saffran, and James Warwick.

Mike Mitchell
New York City
November, 2017

I should hardly come to Newport for the materials of a tragedy. But I can fancy finding here the motive of a drama which should depend more on smiles than tears.

Henry James
Travel Writings
Newport, 1870

From an architectural guide to Newport, Rhode Island:

The evocatively named Windstone, formerly known (from 1895 to 1948) as Winthrop Hall, while not as well-known as many of its contemporaries, is nonetheless regarded as one of the architectural treasures of Bellevue Avenue, and is considered to be a masterpiece of the Beaux-Arts style of architecture.

For more than a century, the ballroom at Windstone was the setting for a succession of lavish entertainments given by the Winthrop/Livingston family. It is one of the few such properties constructed during the Gilded Age that continues to be occupied by descendants of the family for whom it was originally built.

PROLOGUE

No one wanted to be there—except Joanna—and least of all Joanna. The drive down from Providence had been contentious all around. Danny felt that the entire trip was a huge waste of time, a point of view which he expressed repeatedly. It was so typical of Joanna, he said—her impulsive ideas, her moodiness, her ambivalence about her family and her past. Nick and Sara, on the other hand, had simply come along for the ride, during most of which Sara was either defending Joanna against Danny's attacks or trying to entertain Nick—who was bored out of his mind because of having to go 45 minutes without Wi-Fi. Not having the option to play games had plunged him into a kind of withdrawal from violent imagery. A ten car pileup with multiple fatalities along I-95 would have been a godsend for Nick—but there was no such luck.

And now they were stuck in this dreary bar.

The four of them were normally quite at home in bars, but this one had no music, no Wi-Fi, no large flat-screen televisions and, as a result, almost no customers. They had made the mistake of letting Joanna pick the venue. After all, as Danny begrudgingly conceded, it was her birthday. They had all had a few quick pints and finished their burgers—and although Joanna had had several rum and Cokes—her burger was still sitting untouched in front of her, and she was beginning to look somewhat catatonic. In a rare moment of whimsy, Sara produced a large birthday candle, which she stuck into the middle of Joanna's burger. Nick suggested they should light the candle—not out of an observance of convention, but because he liked fire.

"Why bother," said Danny, "She's too fucked-up to notice."

"Should we sing?" asked Sara.

"No singing!" said Danny, in the peremptory way that always got him what he wanted.

Nick lit the candle.

"Aren't you gonna make a wish?" Sara asked.

"There's no cake," said Joanna, who hadn't spoken for a while.

"You don't like cake," said Danny.

"I like birthday cake," said Joanna.

"Who knew?" said Danny to the others, in a manner that clearly conveyed "Who the hell ever knows what this nut job likes?"

"Well, you should've known," said Joanna, "I said I didn't like *birthdays*. But I like birthday *cake*."

"Whatever," said Danny, blowing out the candle. "I want another beer." Then, yelling at the waitress, "Yo! Can we get three more beers over here?"

"I want one too," said Joanna.

"You've had enough," said Danny.

"But it's my birthday," said Joanna.

"Oh, so now you like birthdays?" said Danny.

"I don't know what I like," said Joanna, who was beginning to stare into the abyss. Even as she was crumbling inwardly, however, there remained an outward vestige of something about Joanna Cushing that tended to elevate her above her companions—an outmoded kind of dignity, a sense of decorum, and the illusion of self-possession. Even so, she had been leading an aimless, dissolute life for so long now that she tended to think of herself as being on their level.

She was in her mid-thirties and had the kind of natural beauty that nothing seemed to impair—a consideration which was of paramount importance to Danny. Joanna had begun to think of Danny as a one night stand that had lasted five years—whereas, for him, she was a trophy girlfriend who had become more trouble than she was worth. He was the owner of the bar where she played piano on weekends. Nick was Danny's best friend, as well as being Joanna's drug dealer, and Sara was—well, she was simply Sara. She had no ambition in any direction—no discernible purpose in life—and yet she was the best of a bad lot.

While Danny was busy bribing the waitress to bring one more rum and Coke to the table, Joanna took a handful of pills from her bag and, unseen by the others, swallowed them with a gulp of Danny's beer.

"Alright," said the waitress, who had monitored Joanna's descent with the jaded eye of a middle-aged barmaid, "She can have one more. But then you take her home."

"We shoulda stayed in Providence," Nick blurted out unhelpfully, as he was inclined to do.

"This is my hometown!" said Joanna, galvanizing what little indignation she could still manage to summon.

"Yeah, right," said Danny, "and you haven't been here for like what—twenty years?"

Spying an old upright piano near the bar, Sara saw another opportunity for diplomacy.

"Hey, Jo! There's a piano," she said, "Why don't you play something?

"I don't want to play the piano," Joanna replied.

"Aw, come on," said Nick, desperate for any relief from boredom.

"I don't want to play the fucking piano!"

"What if I promised to get you one more drink for the road?" said Nick.

"Dude!" Danny snapped at him, "Seriously?"

Looking toward Sara through the haze, and vaguely perceiving someone she regarded as a positive specimen of humanity, Joanna decided to relent. With laborious attempts to steady herself, she got up and walked over to the piano. Taking hold of the piano for support, she noticed the handsome bartender, and smiled poignantly at him. He smiled cheerfully back at her. As the waitress was about the take Joanna's drink to the piano, the bartender stopped her.

"I've got this one," he said, moving the drink to the end of the bar that was nearest the piano.

Joanna seated herself precariously at the piano, slowly lifted the keyboard cover, and stared at the keys in a haunted sort of way. Then she began playing a Chopin Prelude. It was Op. 28, No. 7—a melancholy piece at the best of times, but all the more so when played at the dirgelike tempo that was all she could manage under the circumstances.

The performance drew a mixed reception. The waitress looked quite impressed, and the bartender looked downright mesmerized. But Joanna's companions, who had only ever heard her play their favorite pop tunes, seemed to take it as a personal affront.

"What the fuck is that, Jo?" said Danny, "What is that?"

"It's Chopin," Joanna said.

"What's that supposed to mean?" Danny replied, "What the fuck is show pan?"

"Come on, Jo," said Nick, "play something."

"I *am* playing something!" Joanna replied loudly and angrily, which she then repeated, quietly and pathetically and mostly to herself, "I *am* playing something."

"Well, it sucks," said Nick.

Undaunted by the negative reviews from her companions, Joanna finished the short piece and stepped up to the bar to claim her reward. The bartender was still smiling, and he and the waitress both applauded, as Joanna attempted to take a bow.

"That was beautiful," he said.

"All I wanted was to go home for my birthday," was Joanna's slurred response. As she reached for her drink, it became clear to the bartender that she was about to pass out, and he caught her just in time.

A few hours later, as the fluorescent lights of the emergency room began to overrule the darkness she had been seeking, Joanna could hear the voice of a nurse, explaining to a doctor that his patient now seemed a little more coherent.

"She knows her name now," she told the doctor, "and who the president is."

"How are you feeling, Joanna," asked the doctor, leaning over the gurney.

"What's going on?" Joanna asked.

"You're in the hospital," said the doctor.

"Am I in Providence?"

"No, you're in Newport."

"Why am I in the hospital?"

"Well—it looks as if you tried to kill yourself."

For a few moments, there was nothing. Then there were vague recollections. It wasn't a total blackout this time. Something about a car trip. Something about a bar. Something about a bunch of pills and a smiling bartender. Something about Chopin. A dimly recalled series of events culminating in a feeling of hopelessness and despair. Tears began streaming down her cheeks, and all she could say was "Oh, God."

—1—

The Newport Women's Rehabilitation Center was housed in a mid-Victorian mansion, in what had once been—before being eclipsed by the unbridled opulence of the Gilded Age—the fashionable end of Bellevue Avenue. Owing to a perennial lack of adequate funding, the mansion's once celebrated beauties had long since begun to deteriorate, although they remained evident to the discerning eye. Most of the women who were housed there saw nothing around them but a moldering heap of Victorian gloom—but Joanna Cushing had a discerning eye. She recognized the faded William Morris wallpaper, the paneled staircases and ubiquitous wainscoting of Stanford White, and the oak garlands carved in the style of Grinling Gibbons that adorned the mantelpieces. All of it aroused in her an acute sense of appreciation mixed with a profound sense of sadness—but then, Joanna had mixed reactions to everything. She had been a seriously devoted music major at school but, doubting her potential as a musician, had minored with an almost equal enthusiasm in art history. And the three months she'd spent in rehab reminded her that, for anyone interested in art, architecture, and history—Newport, Rhode Island is a treasure trove.

After a late winter and early spring filled with 12-step meetings, group and individual therapy sessions, and various assigned tasks, she began to go out for short walks. At first, she would walk around 'The Point,' the beautifully preserved colonial district just to the northwest. As the weather improved, she would sometimes venture on foot over the causeway that led to Goat Island. Then, as her moods began to match the weather, she accepted her roommate's standing offer for the use of a bicycle.

Now she could ride south along Thames Street, and on to Fort Adams, Castle Hill and Brenton Point, taking in the spectacular views of Narragansett Bay. Eventually, she would ride along Ocean Avenue up to the point where it connected with the far end of Bellevue Avenue, the place called Rough Point, where she would always stop abruptly, consider going on, and decide instead to return the same way she had come. That stretch of Bellevue beyond Rough Point contained the foremost splendors of the Gilded Age—the great summer palaces that proclaimed wealth beyond imagining. It was in one of those great mansions—a house called Windstone—that Joanna had been born thirty-five years earlier, and where her sole surviving relative, her grandmother, still lived; and it was for that reason that Joanna denied herself the pleasure of continuing on. Besides, it was not as if the lesser palaces along Ocean Avenue were anything to sniff at. In any case, depending on the way she viewed the world on a given day, Joanna vacillated between disparaging the splendors that surrounded her as monuments to rapacity and conspicuous consumption—or simply delighting in them for their undeniable beauty.

On what she assumed would be her last spin around the island, she returned to the rehab to find a note summoning her, at her earliest convenience, to the administrator's office. The day she had been dreading had finally come. She would soon have to return to Providence—to Danny, Nick and Sara—at least for the time being. After that, she knew everything would have to change; otherwise she would not be able to stay sober and drug-free. Danny, no doubt, would have paid for the rehab, and would be expecting a return on his investment—the nature of which would be determined entirely by him. Yes, everything would have to change. For now, though, she walked forlornly, like a wounded child, toward the administrator's office.

Helen Thomas, the administrator of the Women's Rehabilitation Center, was a woman in her late fifties who, having survived several decades of involvement with alcoholics and addicts—including both of her husbands—considered herself to be a worldly and supremely self-confident woman. As the staff members were fond of saying, and she was fond of hearing, "Nothing could rattle Helen." When she could spare the time (which was anytime she was asked), Helen played leading roles in amateur theatrical productions and, as such, was something of a local diva. All of that being the case, she was taken aback by the sudden awareness that she felt quite intimidated by the young woman now sitting in front of her.

Yes, Joanna was young and beautiful—but it couldn't be that. And Helen had long since gotten over being impressed with Joanna's famous family—so it couldn't be that. Or could it? In fact, it was all of that, but it was something else as well. When Joanna was feeling insecure, she had an unsettling way of looking at strangers that made them feel as though she were penetrating and judging their innermost thoughts. There was no malice in this; there was barely even any awareness of it because, to a degree, it was inbred. Mostly, though, it was the means Joanna had unconsciously developed of shielding herself from her own lack of self-worth by putting others on their guard.

At first, Helen fidgeted with Joanna's file, pretending to study it, despite the fact that she was thoroughly familiar with its contents.

"So—you are—let's see here—Joanna Cushing?" she said, as if seeing the name for the first time.

"Yes."

"And you're leaving us tomorrow?"

"Yes."

"And—let's see here—" said Helen (still pretending to unearth familiar details), "your grandmother is—Mrs. Livingston?"

"Yes."

"Louisa Winthrop Livingston?"

Before she could stop herself, Helen had said the name with a degree of reverence that she had not intended to reveal, even to herself. It was a tone that was irritatingly familiar to Joanna.

"Yes, obviously!" said Joanna. "You sent for me, didn't you?"

"Of course, of course," said Helen, who was now on the verge of being disconcerted, but she quickly recovered.

"I was just confirming that our records are accurate. Shall we just get down to business, then?"

"Please," said Joanna.

"I assume your counselor has told you we've been in touch with your grandmother?"

"No."

"Well, it seems," said Helen, "that your grandmother has arranged to pay your outstanding bill—*and* she's agreed to let you stay with her for the time being."

"I'm sorry," said Joanna, as though she hadn't heard what had just been said, "I didn't mean to snap at you before. It's got nothing to do with you, obviously. Everyone's been so nice to me here. It's just that—I haven't had anything to do with my family for a very long time."

"I see," said Helen. "I wasn't aware of that."

Then, after a bit of random paper shuffling to allow for the prolonged stage pause Helen liked to insert before the finale, she continued.

"You know, after twelve weeks in rehab, the outside world is going to be very difficult for you to adjust to without drugs and alcohol."

"Yes," said Joanna, "I'm sure."

"I think it might be especially hard for you. I mean, you nearly killed yourself—not that long ago—and now you have no home, no job, no family really. I mean, your parents—"

Helen stopped for a moment, noting the discomfort the reference had caused for Joanna. When Joanna was a teenager, her mother and step-father had both drowned in a boating accident and, even in therapy, she'd never talked about it.

"I'm sorry to bring that up," said Helen, "but it did get an awful lot of media coverage at the time."

"Yes, it did," said Joanna.

"Well," said Helen, feeling that a positive note needed to be struck, "you still have a lot going for you. I mean, you're still young, you're quite attractive, you have an excellent education, and you have at least one very influential relative. You can probably make a life for yourself—I mean, with all of that going for you."

"Yes, well, *going* seems to be the operative word there," said Joanna.

"Alright then," said Helen, "are you all packed and ready to go?" She said this as insensitively as if she were suddenly running a supermarket checkout, but it was only because she couldn't think of anything else to say.

"As ready as I'll ever be," said Joanna.

"And, are you able to drive? No restrictions?"

"You mean like a DUI or something? No, nothing like that. The only restriction is that I don't have a car."

"I see. Well, we'll get you a taxi."

"No, that's okay," said Joanna, "It's a short walk, and I don't have much stuff."

After asking Joanna to sign some papers, Helen thanked her, wished her good luck, and smiled at her in a way that conveyed a modicum of warmth while also indicating an end to the proceedings. After Joanna left the room, Helen gave herself a big mental pat on the back for not allowing what remained of her schoolgirl infatuation with high society to have revealed itself—at least not for any longer than it had taken her to say an old woman's name.

—2—

The next afternoon, Joanna stuffed the few items of clothing Danny (or more likely Sara) had sent down from Providence into a large backpack, and set out for what she expected to be a short walk to Windstone. But the distances between the houses along Bellevue were greater than she remembered, and the walk took much longer than expected. Even so, it was not a disagreeable experience. Soon after leaving the rehab, she passed the Newport Casino and entered the so-called mansion district, where Gilded Age mansions dominate the avenue. In addition to the architectural spectacle, the warm spring air was perfumed with a mixture of flowering trees and reawakening gardens which, when mixed with a refreshing breeze from the Atlantic side of the island, created an almost utopian sense of harmony and well-being. Alas, it wasn't long before that sense of well-being was replaced by a familiar knot in Joanna's stomach.

Even after an absence of eighteen years, she could feel, almost viscerally, the proximity of Windstone. It was not a place one could easily forget, even if one hadn't spent one's childhood summers there. To begin with, from a distance, there were the massive limestone walls. As was typical of Bellevue Avenue, the walls had been made high enough to seem forbidding, while still providing tantalizing views of the splendor that lay behind them. When Joanna finally arrived at the wrought-iron gates (which were never closed), she stood for a moment, taking in what motorists observe only in a fleeting glimpse—the meticulously cobbled courtyard, the imposing porte cochère, and the great central hall from which the house had taken its original name of Winthrop Hall, and which rose majestically above the Italianate façade. While not the most palatial of the Newport 'summer cottages,' Windstone was nonetheless considered one of the most beautiful—and a paragon of the Beaux-Arts style.

Stepping inside the gate, Joanna was able to take in the things that no motorist—nor even the infrequent pedestrian—could catch a glimpse of: the meticulously arranged classical statuary, the fluted pilasters, and the exquisitely sculpted bas-relief along the wall. (An interviewer had once written that Louisa Livingston's ancestors had left no stone uncarved.) Along the interior of the walls was perhaps the finest herbaceous border on this side of the Atlantic. It had been inspired by the famous one at Hardwick Hall in Derbyshire—and it was Louisa Livingston's pride and joy. Any element within view would have been enough to arrest one's attention, but it was the harmony of the ensemble for which Windstone was justly famous. The overall effect was one of an earthly paradise—or, in the mindset of its current occupant—an apotheosis of impeccable taste.

Joanna would have loved to remain there and savor the beauty of the place, but the knot in her stomach reminded her that this was no time for art appreciation. Walking as slowly as possible, she crossed the courtyard and rang the doorbell. After what seemed to her like a lengthy interval (although it was barely more than a minute), a somewhat elderly looking man opened the door. Joanna recognized him as Harris, the English butler who had served her grandmother for decades.

"Yes?" he said glacially, in the supercilious manner of his profession. English butlers are not in the habit of greeting even the most familiar visitors with a warm smile and a slap on the back, but young women arriving at the front entrance to the house wearing jeans and tee-shirts were neither a familiar nor a welcome occurrence.

"Hello, Harris," said Joanna, "It's nice to see you."

"May I help you?" he replied frigidly, slightly affronted by the familiarity.

"Harris—it's Jo," said Joanna, removing her hat and her large sunglasses. "Isn't my grandmother expecting me?"

Harris had been more or less expecting someone who looked like a young Jackie Kennedy, perhaps wearing a pillbox hat, with matching patent-leather shoes and handbag.

"Oh, I'm so sorry, Miss," he said. "Do come in, please. Mrs. Livingston is having her tea at present, but I'll take you to your room—so that you might, uh, freshen up."

Joanna stepped into the Great Hall.

Her main memory of the hall had been as a place where she had roller-skated as a child—but her adult eye now perceived it for the masterpiece it truly was. It was the kind of massive interior where staircases on either side, or one grand staircase in the center, would have been customary. Instead, the architect had designed a staircase to the right—and the stairs, bordered by a lacy wrought-iron balustrade, increased in width as they curved gracefully toward the bottom, giving the square hall a slight feeling of curvature. On the wall along the staircase were portraits of several generations of Winthrops and Livingstons. On the wall opposite the stairs were two enormous paintings thought to be by Rubens, depicting orderly scenes of ancient violence. These giant canvasses were bordered on either side and in between by tall marble pedestals supporting Roman busts. Below each of the paintings was a long gilt Venetian settee, upholstered in a rich coral silk. The marble floor was of a broad black and white checked pattern, diagonally set, which reflected beautifully in the immense gilt mirrors that hung on either side of the front door, as one descended the stairs. Above it all, hanging from the rotunda, was the largest 18th century rock crystal chandelier anyone could imagine.

"How on earth," Joanna asked herself "did I ever take all this for granted?"

"This way, please," said Harris, indicating the direction of the staircase.

As they crossed the hall, Joanna's sneakers made a squeaking sound against the marble floor—which Harris appeared not to have noticed even when she apologized for it. Passing by an open door to their right, the voice of an elderly woman suddenly shot out at them.

"Harris! Who is that?" said the old woman, "Is that my granddaughter?"

Reflexively, Harris redirected Joanna through the open door of the room, which was the library.

The library was the room where Louisa Livingston now essentially lived her life. Besides being an avid reader, she took most of her meals there, received her few callers there, conducted all of her business from the library desk, and occasionally (though always unintentionally) napped there.

The last time Joanna had seen her grandmother, she was a woman of regal bearing in her sixties, courteous yet intimidating, and with boundless energy. From what she could tell at a glance, the only thing likely to have changed in almost twenty years was Louisa's level of energy, and even that wasn't yet certain. She sat bolt upright, wearing a vintage Chanel suit and pearls, impeccably groomed, flanked by a formal afternoon tea service, over which she presided, even when she was alone, with the formality of a Geisha. She was, in every sense, a creature from another era. In contemporary terms, she might as well have been a rare species of bird in some remote rainforest.

"Miss Cushing, Madam," said Harris, standing in the doorway, then stepping to one side to allow Joanna to enter. Joanna stood almost motionless, only bending slightly from the waist and craning her neck a bit to take in the large, well-appointed room, as though it were a perfunctory stop on a museum visit.

"Hello, Granny. It's good to see you," she said after a few seconds, while still standing in the doorway.

"That's all, Harris," said Louisa, tossing aside a pile of papers that appeared to distress her.

"Very good, Madam" said Harris, squeezing past Joanna, who remained awkwardly rooted in the doorway.

"Joanna," said Louisa, softly at first, and then more firmly. "Joanna!"

"Oh, sorry! I kinda spaced out for a minute—I mean, you know—being here again. And, um, I'm not used to being called Joanna."

"Yes, well, I'm not used to being called Granny, but I know when I'm being spoken to."

Joanna still did not move.

"Would you care to sit?" asked Louisa, making it sound more like a decree than a polite suggestion. Like others of her class and generation, she spoke with a mid-Atlantic accent augmented with Anglicisms.

Joanna seated herself on a settee that faced the matching settee on which Louisa sat. Suddenly, she became aware that she hadn't yet taken off her backpack, which she now nervously removed and tossed gently onto the floor. In Louisa's world, this was no less ill-mannered than flinging a dead mouse onto the carpet—but, in Louisa's world, one took no discernable notice of such things.

"What do people call you if not Joanna?" she asked.

"Um—people usually call me Jo."

"Hmm. Your mother used to call you Jo. I thought it suited you at the time. You were a bit of a tomboy."

"I thought it was because she loved *Little Women* so much," said Joanna. "She always said she wanted me to be independent. You know, like Jo in the book."

"Well, she certainly got her wish," said Louisa, making what should have been a compliment feel more like an indictment. She preferred not to be reminded that her own mother had named her after the book's author, Louisa May Alcott—a name which, in the 1930's, everyone thought was 'terribly old-fashioned.'

"I would prefer to call you Joanna—if you don't mind," said Louisa.

"It's my name," said Joanna. "Why would I mind?"

"Precisely," said Louisa, with whom people rarely disagreed. "Now—would you care for a cup of tea? I suppose that sounds rather uninteresting to you. I *would* offer you something stronger, of course, but—"

"Of course," said Joanna, mumbling.

"What's that?" said Louisa, "I didn't hear you."

"I said yes, I'll have some tea," said Joanna, almost shouting.

"That's not what you said," Louisa shot back. "You said something impertinent. I could see it on your face. You probably think I'm losing my hearing because I'm getting old. Well, I am *not* losing my hearing. I can hear you perfectly well when you speak in a proper tone and don't mumble. Nevertheless, how do you take it?"

Joanna appeared confused.

"Your tea?" Louisa added.

"Oh, um, I guess with a little non-fat milk. And some Sweet'n Low, I guess."

"I have cream and sugar," said Louisa.

"Oh, that's fine. A little cream and—some sugar, I guess."

"Would you care to guess how many lumps?"

"Um—a few?"

"How many lumps of sugar would you like?" Louisa asked.

"I don't know," said Joanna feebly. "Five?"

"Have you ever had a cup of tea in your life?" Louisa asked.

"Yes, of course I have," said Joanna, "But not with lumps in it."

"Well, five lumps of sugar in one cup is going to be awfully sweet—but it's your cup of tea."

"Not really," said Joanna, mumbling again under her breath—then adding, more audibly, "They say having sweets helps you detoxify from alcohol, but it's probably just an excuse to indulge."

Louisa did not respond. She was busy ceremoniously pouring the tea, to which she immediately added two lumps of sugar, after which, with a lowering of her eyelids, she slowly, with visible reluctance, added the other three lumps one at a time.

"Now," said Louisa, "will you have a tea sandwich? Or would you rather just have all the cakes and jam?"

"I'm not very hungry," said Joanna (which wasn't true), "and that wasn't very nice."

"No, I don't suppose that was very nice," said Louisa.

As the two women sipped at their tea for a silent spell, Joanna was instantly aware that her tea was nauseatingly sweet, but there was no way she would admit that to her grandmother at that moment.

At length, Louisa placed her cup on the table and began to scrutinize Joanna as though she were inspecting a dubious specimen at a vegetable stand.

"How old are you?" she asked. "You must be about thirty by now."

"About," Joanna answered glumly. Age was not her favorite topic.

"When I was your age, I was maintaining three large houses—the one in New York, the one in Palm Beach, and this one—*and* I had to cope with about twenty servants."

Joanna was tempted to say "I'll bet the servants did most of the coping," but instead she said "That must have been a lot of work," realizing, as the words left her mouth, how insipid they must have sounded.

"Well, yes it was," said Louisa, almost amiably, "but you've missed my point entirely."

"No, I haven't," said Joanna, rather testily. "Your point is that I'm a failure. You made that very clear. But I know I'm a failure. I knew that when I came in."

"*Well*," said Louisa, "I'm not sure what to say to *that*. At least we can agree on something, I suppose."

As Joanna shrugged blithely, Louisa continued.

"The question is—what are you planning to do about it?"

This was Joanna's other least favorite topic. The simple truth was that she had no clue—and she had the poor judgement to share that fact with her grandmother.

"Do you mean to say you have no plans at all?" Louisa began. "No goals? No ambitions? Nothing? Joanna, I don't mean to seem domineering. I'm simply asking what you intend to do with your life." And when no answer was forthcoming, she added, "Isn't there *something* you'd like to do?"

For a moment, Joanna appeared to be giving the question the kind of serious reflection Louisa expected. Then she answered.

"I'd like to take a nap."

After exhaling with considerable frustration, Louisa rang the buzzer that would summon Harris, who materialized about a minute later—although, as before, it seemed far longer to Joanna.

"Harris! My granddaughter wishes to have a nap," said Louisa. She said this with the same bemusement she might have expressed if she'd said that her granddaughter had just converted to cannibalism. Harris was in the process of reaching for Joanna's backpack, and preparing once again to show her to her room, when Louisa asked him to step outside the door for a moment and close it behind him, after which she decided to drop the veneer of courtesy that she alone felt she had maintained up to now.

"Look here," she began, "I'm not at all happy about this arrangement. You're my granddaughter, and I feel some responsibility toward you, but I will not support any sort of degenerate behavior. I've—I've been through this sort of thing before, you see—with your mother. She made a complete mess of her own life and then—well, it appears she didn't teach you the things a mother ought to teach a daughter. Of course, I don't suppose she could teach what she didn't know herself."

"Well, she learned everything from you," said Johanna—proving, if nothing else, that she was her grandmother's granddaughter.

Louisa winced.

"You'd better have that nap now," she said. "We can continue this discussion at dinner."

"Great," said Joanna, grabbing her backpack and heading for the door, "I can't wait."

When Joanna had left the room, Louisa made an effort to compose herself by retrieving the packet of papers she had tossed aside earlier, forgetting for the moment about the dire news they contained. Then, realizing that she was too distracted by her reunion with her granddaughter to focus on anything else, she tossed the papers aside again, covered her face, and began to cry. On the very rare occasions when Louisa cried, she always covered her face—as if she were ashamed to cry, even when alone.

In the meantime, Harris had taken Joanna to the top of the stairs, where he stopped in front of the first door to the right of the landing. Joanna continued to walk until he cleared his throat in the distinctive way butlers do when they have something uncomfortable to say.

"That's alright, Harris," she said, "I still remember where my room is—believe it or not."

"Mrs. Livingston thought you might be more comfortable here, Miss—in the Blue Room."

"Really?" said Joanna, "Isn't that normally reserved for very special guests?"

"That's right, Miss," said Harris.

"Or—maybe just people she wants to keep an eye on. That's her room opposite, isn't it?"

"It is, Miss."

"Well, won't that be cozy?"

"Surely Mrs. Livingston considers her nearest relative to be a very special guest," said Harris.

"Oh, yeah," said Joanna, "she made that very clear."

Noticing that Harris appeared to be struggling for a way to say something, Joanna asked him if he was alright. He said he was fine, but that her grandmother had not been herself recently—and that she seemed to be under what he called a good deal of stress. He suggested that her age might have something to do with it, and went on to explain that the world Louisa Livingston had belonged to had more or less vanished. He said it was something she hadn't seemed to notice for a long time—but that recently, so many of her friends had passed away, or were ill, or were simply, like herself, withdrawn. He reluctantly added—apologizing in advance for overstepping his position—that whereas Mrs. Livingston had always been assertive, he had never known her, until recently, to cause discomfort in others.

"Look," said Joanna, too enervated to summon up her usual compassion, "no disrespect, Harris, but life is difficult for everyone. Maybe living in the past makes it easier—especially when you've had a past like hers—but it sounds like you're telling me that living in the past isn't working for her anymore and—I'm sorry, but—it's hard to feel sympathy for someone who's always lived on top of the world, especially when you know what the world is like for most people. I appreciate your concern, though, and I'm sure we can talk about it later but—right now—I'm really tired."

"Yes, of course, Miss," said Harris, "I do apologize."

"No—no, it's fine," said Joanna, taking hold of his arm, "You did the right thing—telling me. You're a good man."

"Thank you, Miss," said Harris. "I hope you'll have a pleasant rest. If you need to go out, you'll find a key to the front door on the table next to it. And, if you require anything further, you'll find a buzzer next to your bed."

"I can't imagine requiring anything further," she said, opening the door to her room, then stopping. "Actually, there is one thing you could do for me. You could stop calling me Miss. I'm already painfully aware that I'm single, thank you. Just call me Joanna."

"Oh, I couldn't, Miss," said Harris. "For one thing, Mrs. Livingston would never permit it. She prefers the old ways."

"I'll bet she does," said Joanna. "I'm surprised she doesn't make you wear a powdered wig."

Noticing what seemed like a serious reaction in response to a lighthearted comment, Joanna quickly added that she hoped she hadn't offended him, which he assured her she had not. He said it was just that she had reminded him of something, whereupon he scurried down the stairs with the swiftness of a man half his age.

Being alone in a room of her own for the first time in several years acted as a catalyst for Joanna's pent-up emotions, which seemed to swing back and forth between an unnerving jumble of ill-defined fears and a clearly defined sense of instability, insecurity, and loneliness. She thought about Helen Thomas' admonition, and suddenly felt as if she was adrift at sea with no discernible means of steering. The irony of having a beautifully furnished bedroom the size of Danny's entire apartment was not lost on her, however, and she was able, if nothing else, to feel grateful for having such a beautiful, quiet—and private—room.

Walking across the room as she began to undress, she noticed that the sumptuous furnishings, particularly the heavy brocade curtains and the rich damask upholstery of the chairs, were a little the worse for wear. As she walked in front of the fireplace, she ran a finger along the mantelpiece, revealing more than a thin layer of dust.

The thing about the room which she found the most immediately inviting—besides the bed—was a large set of windows that looked out over a formal garden leading to an expanse of lawn that seemed to merge with the Atlantic on the horizon. Once that *coup d'oeil* moment had passed, however, she noticed that the grounds of Windstone, like the furniture in her room, were in need of care.

Still, taking in the beautiful view and the beautiful day from her beautiful room, Joanna experienced a few moments of peace, and even a sense of safety. Then she remembered the gorgon downstairs. Walking over to the bed, she noticed an odd thing about the Blue Room.

"There's nothing blue in here," she said aloud, "except me," after which she fell sobbing onto the bed—unaware and unsuspecting that the gorgon below was also sobbing—and for some of the same reasons.

—3—

When she had finally managed, after an anxious period of tossing and turning, to doze off for a couple of hours, Joanna heard a knock at the door. It was Harris, announcing that dinner was about to be served. After a brief, frantic effort to improve her appearance, she realized that, no matter how much effort she made, she would still make a poor showing in the eyes of her grandmother—and so she gave it up as a lost cause and headed downstairs.

The room directly across from the library was the opulent formal dining room of Windstone and, as Joanna entered the room, she was surprised that no place settings had yet been laid on the vast dining table. Passing in front of one of a pair of Boulle sideboards that flanked the entrance, she ran a finger over the marble top and, as in her room, left a trace on its dusty surface. Atop the sideboard there was an immense silver salver with several decanters containing alcoholic beverages, which Joanna began fingering mindlessly. As she unconsciously lifted the top off of one of the paler substances, her grandmother walked into the room.

"Do I need to have those locked up?" she said. Without waiting for Joanna's response, she went on. "I'm sorry, I didn't mean to sound harsh. I was simply wondering whether I should have all the alcoholic beverages put away somewhere. For your comfort, of course."

"That's not necessary," said Joanna, "I'm really not tempted."

"As you wish," said Louisa. "I've never understood addictions—but one imagines that temptation should be avoided."

"But, as I said, I'm not tempted," said Joanna, once again in possession of a glimmer of self-assurance.

"Very well then," said Louisa, "Shall we have our dinner?"

"They don't seem to be ready for us yet," said Joanna.

"I don't whom you mean by *they*," Louisa said huffily.

"I mean that the table isn't set," said Joanna, "Or—are we dining out?"

"Oh that," said Louisa, with the closest thing to insecurity Joanna had yet observed in her grandmother—though it was gone in a flash. "I thought we'd just have a tray in the library. I always have a tray in the library when I'm alone."

Louisa said this as if she considered herself to be alone at present, which was not lost on Joanna. Making a gesture which suggested they should leave the room, Louisa walked back into the great hall, but stopped abruptly when she saw an open pair of French doors which were barely visible beyond the staircase.

"Those doors are *not* to be left open!" she said, as if addressing a cadre of cowering servants—after which she strode imperiously toward the open doors, with Joanna in tow. As she proceeded to close them, Joanna was reminded that this was the entrance to the ballroom.

"Do you still use the ballroom much?" she asked.

"Don't be ridiculous," Louisa snapped back. "No one uses their ballroom anymore. Well, I mean, no one can afford to—let alone the fact that there aren't enough people of the right sort even to fill a ballroom anymore."

A few moments later, as they two women entered the library, Harris was already present, having arranged the dinner, and was about to uncork the wine.

"My granddaughter will not be having wine with her dinner, Harris," said Louisa. Harris nodded in deference, although it seemed to Louisa that his deferential nod was aimed more toward her granddaughter than to herself. She turned to Joanna.

"You had a telephone call earlier—while you were napping. Some homosexual, it sounded like. He said he was a close friend of yours—as if that were meant to impress me."

"Did he leave a name?" Joanna asked.

"It's on the desk," Louisa replied.

Joanna walked around the desk, which looked like something that might have been used by Napoleon, and picked up the notepad next to the telephone.

"Oh, good," she said. "It's William. I guess I turned my cell phone off and forgot."

"Well, if that's all settled," said Louisa, "do you suppose we might have our dinner now?"

"Oh, sorry," said Joanna, "I didn't realize you were waiting for me," after which she returned to her tray, thanking Harris as he was leaving the room.

The two women began eating in silence. After a few bites, Joanna spoke.

"William isn't gay, by the way. He's just happy."

Louisa feigned a smile, and they went back to eating in silence, until Joanna once again broke the silence.

"William is my sponsor."

"I'm sorry," said Louisa, "your what?"

"My AA sponsor. Alcoholics Anonymous."

After making an unsuccessful effort to take another bite, Louisa put her utensils down firmly.

"I do wish you wouldn't talk about such things. And thank goodness Harris wasn't in the room."

She appeared to have nothing more to add—and yet, a moment later, after picking up her utensils and putting them down again, she went on.

"When I think that a member of this family would choose

to associate with—I don't even know what to call them. Misfits? Derelicts?"

"Oh, Granny!" said Joanna, "It's not like that anymore. Everyone goes to AA these days. I mean, not every person, obviously, but every type of person."

"Not *every* type of person," said Louisa. "Only very weak people."

"Oh, right, okay," said Joanna.

She made an effort to take another bite of food—but instead put her utensils down in the same manner as her grandmother had done.

"No, you know what? It's not okay!" she said. "Look, I appreciate having a place to stay—I really do—and I know I wasn't exactly invited, but that doesn't mean I'm not grateful. But it also doesn't mean you're entitled to disrespect me. You think it's more attractive to get drunk in a ballroom than it is in a dive bar somewhere? At least in a dive bar there's no pretense. Everyone knows they're there to get drunk."

Joanna picked up her fork, and put it down again.

"And, as for your comments about any friends I may have—gay or otherwise—I'll bet that phone isn't ringing off the hook with invitations for you."

Louisa looked as if she was quite eager to respond—but did not respond.

"And," said Joanna, "from the looks of things, I'm guessing there aren't a lot of visitors here either. Believe me, I was just being nice when I asked if you still use the ballroom."

By this point, it was plain that Louisa's feelings were hurt, and yet she managed to maintain her composure.

"Have you any idea what it costs to maintain a property of this size?" she asked. "No, of course you don't."

"No, of course I don't," Joanna replied. "How could I? Anyway, that's not the point."

She was about to stress what the point was, but decided it wasn't worth the trouble.

"You know what? Let's just eat, she said. "I'm starving."

Then, as she was finally about to take another bite of food, she continued talking instead.

"I'm sorry. I didn't mean to yell at you like that."

"If that's the way you feel—" said Louisa, making a transparently insincere effort to appear unaffected.

"I didn't mean to be disrespectful," said Joanna.

"It makes no difference to me," said Louisa.

"Oh, I don't know about that," said Joanna. "Anyway, I apologize."

A moment later, Louisa appeared to be almost smiling—although it was hard to tell.

"Well," she said, "at least I could hear you when you were scolding me. I lied to you earlier. The fact is—I *am* beginning to have some trouble with my hearing. It's not all fun, you know—getting old."

"No, I'm sure it's not," said Joanna. "I'll try to speak up from now on."

"You needn't coddle me" said Louisa. "I'm not an invalid."

"Oh, for God's sake, Granny!" said Joanna. "I was just trying to be nice."

Louisa pretended not to hear this, because she didn't want to admit how much she appreciated it. Instead of responding, she resumed her dinner in silence. Then, after what she deemed to be a tasteful interval, she spoke up.

"How could you possibly know about what used to go on ballrooms?"

"I didn't say I did," said Joanna. "I just said people also got drunk in ballrooms."

"I know you dismiss the life we led here."

"Oh, and how do you know that?"

"Because that seems to be the viewpoint of your entire generation," said Louisa, "but I'm afraid you've thrown the baby out with the bathwater."

"I don't know what that means," said Joanna.

"It means—in this case—that by throwing away a lifestyle that doesn't appeal to you, you've thrown away civilization in the bargain."

"As far as I know," said Joanna, "I haven't thrown away anything. To be honest, I haven't really given it much thought."

"I'm not sure that a lack of curiosity is any better," said Louisa.

"I didn't say I lacked curiosity," said Joanna, determined to hold her own. "I've—you know—read some of the history of what used to go on here—but I'd probably find it more interesting if you were to tell me about it yourself."

"Don't be silly," said Louisa. "It's perfectly obvious that you're not the least bit interested. You're just trying to be nice again."

"Is that such a bad thing?" Joanna asked.

"No," Louisa conceded. "We may as well be civil. In any case, I wouldn't know where to begin."

"Well, just tell me about—I don't know—some of your famous parties?"

"You make it sound so vulgar," said Louisa. "In any case, one doesn't like to crow about one's accomplishments."

"I would," said Joanna, "if I had any."

"I prefer not to dwell on the past," said Louisa, unconvincingly. "Anyway, you're just trying to change the subject."

"Oh, was there a subject?" said Joanna. "I must've missed that. But I'm serious. I think I would really enjoy hearing about it."

"It wouldn't mean anything to you," said Louisa broodingly.

"Okay, fine—I get it. I can see that you're not in the mood to reminisce. It's totally fine."

To her surprise, Louisa found that she was disappointed by Joanna's nonchalant capitulation.

"It's all so far in the past," she said, in a way that suggested she wished to be prodded further on the subject.

"I like hearing about the past," said Joanna. "Unless it's *my* past."

Louisa didn't seem to hear this response. She took a moment, during which her appearance, and to some degree her entire being, seemed to change—and she began to talk to Joanna as though she were speaking with an old friend.

"D'you know," she began, "the first of ball I ever gave in this house—it must've been fifty years ago—I would have been about your age. We had the Duke and Duchess of Windsor to stay—so naturally they were the guests of honor, and naturally they stayed in the Blue Room. The Duchess loved the Blue Room; although, I think she mentioned every day that there was nothing blue in it. The Duke, on the other hand, didn't seem to love *anything*—except her, of course—and playing golf with my husband. He always seemed to me a rather sad figure. But then, I suppose it would be a wrench to be the former king of England and still be alive.

"D'you know, I've never said this to anyone but—to be perfectly honest—I found the Windsors rather dull. The poor things—I don't think either of them ever had a clever thought."

Then, after taking a moment to inwardly confirm her opinion, she went on.

"Hah! What an awful gossip I've become. Doesn't matter. You probably have no idea who I'm talking about."

"I *have* heard of the Duke and Duchess of Windsor, Granny," said Joanna.

"I don't know," Louisa continued intrepidly, "perhaps you young people have a point. There *were* rather a lot of useless people in one's ballroom. But at least they were *sophisticated* useless people. They knew how to behave and how to dress and what to say and what not to say. They knew about the opera and the ballet and the theatre. They knew the House of Worth, but they also knew about the House of Mirth. Oh—that's rather clever, if I say so myself."

"I don't know anything about the House of Worth." said Joanna.

"Oh, well," said Louisa, "they were only the most beautiful clothes in history of the world, that's all."

"But I *have* read House of Mirth."

"Have you indeed?" asked Louisa.

"I thought it was horribly depressing."

"Yes," said Louisa, almost laughing, "I think we can agree that House of Mirth is a terribly depressing book." Then, as she seemed to be studying Joanna anew, she asked "Do you enjoy reading?"

"Yes, very much."

"Well, that's encouraging. You'll find a great many excellent books in this house."

"Great. Thanks. I'll look forward to that."

"Ah," said Louisa to Harris, who had just reentered the room, "You may as well remove all this. We don't seem to have much of an appetite."

Joanna looked despondently at her food, which she'd barely touched. Once Harris had again left the room, she looked at the open doorway, and then back at her grandmother. She had seen Harris wince at the way her grandmother had said the word homosexual earlier.

"I think he might be gay, you know," she said.

"What?" said Louisa, absentmindedly. "Oh, yes, I suppose he is. Technically, at least. He never goes anywhere. Now look here—I hope you don't think I have a problem with homosexuals because of one offhand remark. I do *not* have a problem with homosexuals."

"I'm glad to hear it," said Joanna.

"In any case, Harris is devoted to me, and he works cheap. Well, not exactly cheap, but for much less than he's worth—not that I could ever put a price on his true worth. And besides, he likes my stories."

"I'll bet you have a lot of them," said Joanna.

"D'you know," said Louisa, taking this as another prompt, "my own grandmother gave her first ball in this house—*in 1895!*"

"Really?" said Joanna.

"The guest of honor was a Russian Grand Duke—if can you imagine that. Now those were the days. That was before it became all about film stars."

"Don't you like actors either?"

"Of course I don't dislike actors! Stop putting words in my mouth. I simply meant to say that everything was different a century ago. After all, it was *La Belle Époque*."

"Oh, yes—The Gilded Age" said Joanna.

"I don't like that term," said Louisa. "It sounds garish. It was called the beautiful epoch for a reason."

Joanna was about to respond, but Louisa continued unabated.

"I remember my grandmother talking about it as if it were yesterday. Can you imagine—a beautiful summer evening—with the sea breezes coming through the ballroom doors? They were always left open so that couples could waltz out onto the terrace. Bouquets of fresh flowers everywhere—champagne—magnificent food—men in white tie—women in their Worth gowns—covered in jewels—tiaras—an orchestra playing all through the night."

She paused to enjoy the images she had conjured up. Then she added:

"And they said I knew how to throw a party! Believe me—we didn't hold a candle to the Belle Epoque."

"But, Granny," said Joanna, without stopping to consider the potential reaction to what she was about to say, "it was only like that for a very few people. I mean—only the tiniest upper crust. Most of humanity was probably close to starvation during the so-called Belle Epoque."

"Oh, really?" said Louisa with sudden vehemence, "And just what do *you* know about it? How dare you sit in judgment! That tiny upper crust certainly left you a brilliant heritage—and look what you've done with it. I don't even want to think what you've done with it. You're not going to advance civilization by wallowing in the gutter, you know!"

Another awkward silence ensued.

At first, Joanna was stunned. Then she began almost shaking in an effort to repress the hurt and anger she was feeling.

"I think I'll go for a walk, if you don't mind," she said, getting up and moving toward the door.

"Why should I mind?" Louisa said blithely, "You're not a prisoner here."

"No," said Joanna, as she passed through the doorway, "But you are!"

4

With no plan in mind except a vague idea that it might involve a bar, Joanna bolted out the front door—remembering just in time that Harris had said there was a key to the door on the table next to it. She knew that all the side streets leading downhill from Bellevue Avenue would wind up at the waterfront—and that's where the bars were to be found. Arriving at the bottom of the hill, without stopping to think, she walked into the first bar she saw.

It was still early in the evening, and the bar was empty except for one small group, who were in the process of settling up and leaving. The absence of other customers could not have been more to Joanna's liking, as she walked to the far end of the bar and seated herself on the furthest barstool. The coveted feeling of isolation, with the promise of anesthetic relief, was very familiar to Joanna—although this time, the all too familiar solution did not feel as promising as it had in the past. Nevertheless, she told herself, relief was at hand—and she would surely soon overcome the fact that it didn't seem as appealing as usual. While she was having this inner dialogue, a handsome bartender was making his way down the bar toward where she sat.

"Well, hello there!" he said under his breath, halfway down the bar. Then, arriving at the end, he asked Joanna what he could get for her.

"I'll have a rum and Coke," she said.

"You got it."

"No, wait. You know what? Hold the rum."

"So, just a Coke, then?"

"Just a Coke."

After bringing her the Coke, the bartender found a number of chores in Joanna's vicinity that seemed to require his immediate attention. He was particularly diligent in wiping and re-wiping the surface of the bar. Although she wouldn't have thought that anything could flatter her at that particular juncture—much less amuse her—she couldn't help responding to his behavior.

"I think you may have missed a spot," she said.

"Sorry," said the bartender, "I didn't mean to be so obvious."

"That's okay," Joanna replied, noticing that she had made him blush. "I like a direct approach—when I like anything."

As her voice trailed off, her eyes began welling up.

"Oh my god," he said. "I'm so sorry. I'm really sorry."

"Oh, no. This has nothing to do with you! I'm the one who should apologize—sitting here crying into my Coke in front of a total stranger."

"Would you rather cry into a beer?" he asked.

"Definitely not," said Joanna.

"How about some more Coke then?"

"Sure. But make it a Diet Coke."

"So—hold the Coke this time?"

"Exactly."

After returning with her drink, the bartender extended his hand and introduced himself. He said his name was Pace but, almost at that same moment, a waitress came out of the kitchen to ask him a question, and distinctly called him Ham, while at the same time giving Joanna an odd look. Once the waitress had disappeared, Joanna discovered that she was interested in having a conversation after all.

"Um, did she just call you Ham?"

"Yeah—my full name is Pace Hamilton, so my boss started calling me Ham, and now everybody here calls me Ham."

"Why do I suddenly wish I was cheese?" Joanna mumbled, more audibly than she had intended. "Oh my god!" she said, "I just said that out loud, didn't I?"

"Yes, you did," he said, "and I thank you for it."

"And that was without the rum!" she said.

"That's easily remedied."

"No, really—that's okay," she said. "I've had enough."

"How about some food?" he said. "I can get them to make you a ham and cheese sandwich."

"Oh, very funny," said Joanna. "I'm sorry, but if a guy who looks like you is called Ham, people are bound to make jokes like that all the time, right?"

"Yeah, sometimes. Mostly around closing time."

"Oh, so you're saying I sound pathetic and desperate?"

"No, no! I didn't mean it that way. Really."

Partly because she wanted to change the conversation, but mostly because she'd barely eaten all day, Joanna decided that a ham and cheese sandwich actually sounded pretty good at that moment and, once that was taken care of, Pace wasted no time in resuming the conversation.

"So—should I just call you Cheese—or are you going to tell me your name?"

"Oh, sorry," she said. "I'm Jo. Well, Joanna actually."

"Do you prefer Jo or Joanna?"

"I think I'm starting to like Joanna."

"That makes two of us."

"Ooh—well played! So—should I call you Ham?"

"No, that's all right. I think you can go with Pace."

"Good," she said, stepping over the double entendre, "I mean, it's not the best nickname."

"I know, right? But my dad has it worse. Everyone calls him Hammy."

"Ooh, definitely worse," said Joanna. "That used to be kind of a Newport thing, didn't it" she asked, "that goofy nickname thing?"

"I guess so. Are you not from around here?"

"That's a long story."

"Really? Sounds like a yes or no question to me."

"Okay—yes *and* no," she said. "I was born here, but I've been away for a really long time. And you?"

"I'm from here—sort of."

"What happened to yes or no?"

"Touché," he said. "Okay—I was *not* born here, but I spend pretty much every summer here. So, um—are you still in school?"

"Aw, thanks," said Joanna, now on the verge of blushing herself. "I've been out of school for a few years now."

"Yeah? Where did you go?"

"Brown. I majored in music. How about you?"

"Me too! I mean Brown, not music. I majored in literature."

"That explains touché."

"Just think," he said, "we could've been friends."

Joanna was fairly sure that Pace was around six or seven, if not ten years younger than herself.

"I doubt it," she said, before she could catch herself. "Anyway, I didn't really have any friends at school. Come to think of it, I don't really have any friends now."

"Are you sure you don't want a beer to cry into?" he said.

"Ouch! Don't bother to pull any punches."

"You don't exactly hold back yourself, you know."

"That's true. Especially tonight. I'm sorry but—it's been a day."

"No worries. Anyway, I didn't mean to be so blunt. It's just that—I'm a bartender—and I meet people in here all the time who *really* don't have any friends—and they don't look like you. And they don't sound like you. And they *never* say hold the rum."

With Pace's patient prodding, while she ate her sandwich, Joanna explained her current career situation—leaving out the alcoholic part. He appeared to be riveted—but of course, she thought, he *would* appear to be riveted. It wouldn't have occurred to her that he might be genuinely interested in her for something other than her looks—or, as was the case, in addition to her looks. She told him about how she had planned to become a classical pianist; and how, after having played only one concert, with disastrous results, she had given up on the idea. She told him she had been playing piano on weekends at a dive bar slash restaurant up in Providence that was owned by her boyfriend. Noticing the look which the word boyfriend had produced on Pace's face, she quickly amended the word to ex-boyfriend, amending Pace's facial expression accordingly. Then, looking at the piano over Joanna's shoulder, Pace had a sudden, strong sense of déjà vu, although he couldn't put his finger on the particulars.

"Have we met before?" he asked.

"It's a little late for a pickup line, don't you think?" she replied.

"No, seriously. Have you been in here before?"

Unaware that this was the bar where she'd had her last drink, Joanna said "No," then added, "not to my knowledge," which sounded coy, but which was in fact a completely honest response. Unable to penetrate the penetrating look on Pace's face, she made an attempt to lighten things up.

"Well, I'm getting better at giving a simple answer to a yes or no question, right? I mean, that was a little more succinct, right?"

"Okay," said Pace, "Here's a simple question. Can I see you sometime? Outside the bar?"

"Oh—that's not a simple question. Not right now."

"Got it. That's cool."

"Anyway," she said, "it's a small town. I'll probably run into you somewhere."

"Yeah, well—a small town can seem very big when you're lonely."

Joanna almost laughed out loud.

"Somehow I can't picture you being lonely," she said.

"I wasn't till now," he said without thinking.

Now he was blushing more than ever.

"Okay, now it's my turn to say 'Did I just said that out loud?'"

"Yes, you did," she said, "and I thank you for it."

They both smiled—the insecure way people smile when they need an encore and haven't got one. Joanna, being more aware of that fact than Pace, and suddenly feeling vulnerable, decided that it was time to make her exit.

"Hey," she said abruptly, "this was fun, but—"

"You're not leaving?" said Pace, looking a bit startled and downhearted.

"I think I'd better."

"Is it something I said?"

"Not at all! What do I owe you?

"A second chance?"

"Seriously, how much do I owe you?"

"Seriously, nothing."

"Well then, I guess I'll just have to buy you dinner someday."

"And I guess that would be great," said Pace, visibly relieved.

"You got it," said Joanna.

As she left, reflexively reaching for her purse, she realized she had not brought it with her.

—5—

Strolling back toward Windstone far more calmly and slowly than she had fled from it, Joanna found that she was able to reconsider her situation, particularly after stopping in a small park to call her sponsor William.

"William!" she almost shouted, as soon as he answered the phone, "My grandmother is heinous!"

But by the end of the conversation, with the little information he had to go on, William had conjectured a number of things that might explain her grandmother's behavior. Conceding the fact that the morass of insecurities with which she herself was struggling may have temporarily blindsided her, it hadn't occurred to Joanna that a woman like her grandmother might be having troubles of her own. They were both proud, sometimes obstinate women—something they could easily see in each other—yet not so easily see in themselves. They were also far more vulnerable than they were willing to acknowledge—none of which made anything easier. William agreed that her grandmother had behaved badly toward Joanna, but suggested a number of possible motives for it, including "for want of a better way of putting it," the possibility that it could just be a matter of "getting off on the wrong foot." He knew full well that he was oversimplifying things, but he also knew that Joanna had a tendency to overcomplicate things.

Arriving back at the house, Joanna removed her shoes and quietly crossed the hall, noticing with relief that the library door was closed. As she was about to climb the stairs, she noticed that the ballroom doors were once again open, and decided to do a good deed by closing them. As she went to do so, she saw a concert grand piano at the far end of the room and, instead of closing the doors, walked across the room and sat down at the piano and began what she called "doodling" on the keys. To her surprise, the piano was dust-free and seemed to be in tune. Without thinking any further, she began playing Chopin's Barcarolle.

Almost from the downbeat that begins the piece, she was lost to the world—and therefore didn't notice when Louisa arrived in the doorway, where she remained transfixed. Midway through the piece, however, Joanna looked up at the mirrored walls, saw her grandmother's reflection, and abruptly stopped playing.

"Oh, no!" said Louisa, "Please don't stop."

"I can't remember the next part," said Joanna.

"Now, you know that's not true," said Louisa, crossing the room to the piano. "I'm sorry if I made you self-conscious. I can go away if you like."

While Joanna was wondering how she should respond, Louisa continued.

"It's a good thing I keep this instrument tuned," she said. "It seems like an extravagance these days, but—that was Chopin, wasn't it?"

"Yes," said Joanna.

"How beautiful," said Louisa in far off sort of way. Then, realizing it was up to her to keep the conversation going, she said, "Joanna—if you can play Chopin—why would you ever want to do anything else?"

"Well, that's just it," said Joanna, "I can't play Chopin."

"What do you mean you can't? I just heard you."

"What you just heard wasn't what I just heard."

"No—naturally not."

Sensing that Louisa had been reassessing their situation as well, Joanna decided to risk bringing up a sensitive topic.

"My father loved Chopin, you know."

"He was your stepfather!" said Louisa—echoing, for a moment, her imperious tone from earlier in the evening.

"He was the only father I ever knew," said Joanna.

"Yes," said Louisa, softening her tone, "I suppose that's true."

"You really hated him, didn't you?" said Joanna.

Not wanting to resurrect a combative environment, Louisa gave the question a moment of consideration before responding.

"Oh, I don't know—I don't think I hated *him* exactly. I certainly hated the way he insinuated himself into everything. And the way he took advantage of your mother and encouraged her drinking and—the way he spent all her money. And then," she hesitated, but could see that Joanna knew where she was going. "And then—taking her out on a sailboat in a storm when they were both intoxicated. Well, it was no surprise to me that it ended in tragedy. As far as I was concerned, it began as a tragedy."

Joanna looked puzzled. Louisa could see that she would have to spell it out.

"I mean," she said, trying to sound matter-of-fact without sounding judgmental, "it was perfectly obvious that he was a homosexual."

"Oh God," said Joanna. "Is that why you have a thing about gay people?"

"I do not have a *thing* about gay people!" said Louisa. "Before your stepfather came along, I had no opinion on the subject whatsoever. We never used to talk about such things, you know. Times were different then."

"Exactly. Times were different then," said Joanna. "People had to hide who they were—and not just gay people, by the way. Anyway, my mother loved him, and he loved her—and they were devoted to each other."

"Yes, I suppose that's also true," said Louisa.

She'd given the matter a great deal of thought over the years, but she had resisted arriving at the simple, obvious conclusion Joanna had just put forth—and she couldn't help admiring Joanna's generosity toward her parents—especially when one considered that those parents had neglected Joanna for most of her childhood.

"You're right, of course," said Louisa. "You know, it's ridiculous to drag the same chains along all through life, isn't it? But we do, don't we? And—you must understand, Joanna—I've spent my entire life around the most hardened conservatives. Although, that's no excuse at my age."

That thought made Louisa sigh. Thinking about the past or the future always made her sigh—so she chose instead to think about the present.

"But why are we talking about this when we could be talking about more pleasant things—like your beautiful playing?"

"Pleasant things?" said Joanna. "That subject is a minefield for me."

"*Really?*" said Louisa incredulously, "I simply can't imagine. I should think it would be an absolute joy."

"No offense, but—you're right—you *can't* imagine, and I really don't want to talk about it."

"Now, that's not fair. You made me talk about my past when I'd rather not," said Louisa, ignoring the skeptical reaction on Joanna's face. "Look here, Joanna. I know a good deal about music. Not like you, of course, but I know it takes years of dedication to play the way you do—and you can't tell me you want to simply walk away from all that."

"Oh, Granny, it isn't just up to me," said Joanna. "There are so many other people involved—people who make decisions about who gets a career and who doesn't. People who just—didn't think I was good enough."

"But there are always things that can be done," said Louisa.

"Maybe in your world. Not in mine," said Joanna. "For one thing, that dedication you talked about comes at a much higher price for a woman. Anyway, it's a moot point, because I only gave one concert, and the reviews were—well let's just say they weren't encouraging."

"Oh, my dear, I'm so sorry. That must have been devastating for you. But you seem very—well—you seem almost cavalier about it."

"Yes, well, that's the way I deal with heartbreak and humiliation. Unless there are drugs handy."

"Yes, I understand that. I mean, not the drugs, of course, but I certainly know what it's like to feel that one has to put up a shield. Look, I don't mean to weaken your resolve—at least, I don't think I do—but you must know that most people would give their right arm to play the way you do."

"It'd be kinda difficult to play piano without your right arm," said Joanna.

"Now, stop that. You know what I mean. Most people would give anything to be able to play as beautifully as you do. I know I would."

"Well, I could always give you lessons."

"Oh, yes, and by the time I'm a hundred years old, I could play *Three Blind Mice*."

"Better late than never," said Joanna.

Louisa was about to say that whoever coined that phrase had no idea how late "late" can be, but she was sensing the beginning of a welcome and much needed relationship with her granddaughter, and she didn't want to do or say anything to spoil it. And so, for the first time since her husband was still alive, she simply smiled and shrugged in agreement.

She hadn't realized how long it had been since she had talked to anyone about personal things—but she began to do so now. She told Joanna that, during her childhood and adolescence, she had wanted to be a ballerina, but that her feet were too big. Joanna countered by saying that her biggest problem with the piano was that her hands were too small. Louisa joked that the women in their family seemed to get all the wrong appendages. They both laughed at this, but Joanna could see the sadness behind Louisa's laugh. She asked Louisa if she had ever considered any other career. After a moment of hesitation, she said that, for a long time, she had wanted to be a writer.

"Well, that sounds exciting. Did you ever write anything?"

"I spent two very happy years—my pregnancy and the first year of your mother's life—writing what I thought was a brilliant novel."

"And?"

"And—my husband very bravely sent it to a friend of his who happened to be one of the top publishers in the country."

"And?"

"And I was told—diplomatically—that it was hopelessly old-fashioned, mainly because of my—I think he called it my archaic use of language. You see, I thought that if you called yourself a writer, elevated language still mattered. Anyway, it was probably just as well. I knew your grandfather disapproved of it. He felt that writing fiction would somehow undermine our social position, and of course he was right."

With that, regret and sadness eclipsed Louisa's newfound optimism, and it was her turn to sound cavalier.

"But what does any of that matter now?" she said. "Language is dead. Music is dead."

"Are they?" said Joanna.

"Aren't they?" said Louisa.

"Well," said Joanna, willing to concede the point to a degree, "I guess we don't exactly live in a golden age when it comes to those things."

"We certainly do not," said Louisa. She spoke firmly, but moderated her tone, because she felt she mustn't overwhelm this precious moment of agreement concerning things about which they both cared so deeply.

"Joanna—dear—we've become almost total strangers, you and I. And yet, we're the only real family we have left. I'm—I'm truly sorry for the way I treated you this afternoon."

"Oh, it's alright," said Joanna, shifting uncomfortably.

"No, don't say it was alright—because it wasn't. I'm sure you were frightened enough when you arrived, without me flying around the house on a broomstick."

"I probably deserved it," said Joanna.

"Of course you didn't deserve it," said Louisa. "It had nothing to do with you. You just caught me at a very bad moment. I'd just gotten some—very bad news."

"I thought I was the bad news."

"Not at all, my dear. And I'm sorry I was so defeatist about things just now but—well—those are things that I used to care about so deeply."

"I understand, Granny. Believe me, I'm not the most contemporary girl myself. But—well—things are always changing, aren't they? That doesn't mean they're dead. I mean—music evolves—art evolves—language and literature evolve."

Louisa disagreed inwardly, and was about to state that, in her opinion, Joanna was merely expressing the optimism of youth, but opted instead for the novel experience of not derailing a discussion with her impossibly high ideals.

"Well," she said, "You have every reason to be optimistic. You're young and smart and beautiful—and you have talent. The only talent I ever had was for throwing silly parties."

"It sounds like that was the only talent you were allowed to explore," said Joanna.

The simple truth of this observation landed with much more force than Joanna had intended, and Louisa began to cry. Joanna got up from the piano to give her grandmother a hug. Louisa was not accustomed to being hugged in anything other than a superficial manner and, for a moment, she stiffened—but soon she returned the embrace, fully and wholeheartedly. Still, the level of intimacy which Joanna had so quickly brought into her life, while it made her grateful, made her feel uneasy as well. Without intending to do so, Joanna had unearthed a long-buried past.

"I think I could use a glass of brandy right about now," said Louisa. "You wouldn't mind terribly, would you? It wouldn't make you too uncomfortable?"

"Not at all," said Joanna, "Would that be in the library?"

"If you're sure you don't mind," said Louisa.

"Not at all," said Joanna, taking her grandmother's arm as if they were out for a stroll, and leading her out of the ballroom—and taking care, with a conspiratorial smile, to close the ballroom doors.

As Joanna seated herself in the library, Louisa took a photograph in an ornate silver frame from among a cluster of similarly framed photographs, and handed it to Joanna. The photograph, taken in the 1920s, showed a woman dressed for a costume ball, wearing a powdered wig and an 18th century gown—a woman who looked remarkably like Joanna—which explained Harris's odd reaction to her joke about a powdered wig, as well as a momentarily startled look she thought she'd seen on Louisa's face when they had met earlier in the day.

"That's a photograph of my mother, Lila Winthrop," said Louisa, pouring herself a large snifter of brandy. "When I was a child, I was obsessed with that photograph. I thought my mother was some sort of goddess—although I can't remember her when she actually looked like that. I saw very little of her until I was a grown woman myself. That was how Lila wanted it. She was always embarrassed by me. In her better moods, she called me her little ugly duckling. In her darker moods, she blamed me for ruining her body and causing her to age prematurely. It never occurred to her that her drinking and smoking and—well, all the rest of it—were the reasons she lost her looks. Thank heaven for my own granny. She was more of a mother to me than Lila ever could have been. You know—the women in this family have quite a history of addiction. Maybe that's the reason I was so hard on you earlier. All those painful memories came rushing back. It's odd that I said I knew nothing about addiction. I ought to be an expert. And to think—if only my mother—or your mother—had had the courage to do something about their problems the way you have. That would've been wonderful."

When the evening had begun, the idea of receiving praise from her grandmother, particularly in support of her recovery from addiction, had seemed impossible to Joanna—and although she had always been more comfortable with criticism than praise, she was deeply moved by it now. She shuddered to think that, a short while earlier, she had almost started drinking again because of her unwanted dependence on a woman she had evidently misjudged. While Joanna was lost in such reflections, Louisa was trying to focus her thoughts, with a little help from the brandy.

"Joanna," she said, after a very pregnant pause, "I need to talk to you about something serious."

"Oh, so we're done with the frivolous part of the conversation?" Joanna said.

"Don't make a joke, dear. Not just now" said Louisa, "As I said, I had some bad news today, just before you arrived." It was onerous for her to say what she felt she must say, but she persevered. "The crux of it is that—well—that I'm—I'm not going to have very much money to leave you. Things have gone rather badly for me lately, and—"

"Oh, Granny, stop!" said Joanna. "I don't care about that. I never expected any money from you anyway."

"But you have every right to expect it," said Louisa. Then, relapsing into an hauteur that may or may not have been exacerbated by the brandy, she added, "After all, you're the last descendent from the union of two great families."

"Well, yes, but—actually, come to think of it—I think you should just leave everything to Harris. I mean, he's earned it. I haven't."

"Yes, that's what I was thinking of doing—but now that you're here, everything feels different. Of course, I'll leave him as much as I can. And the two of you could sell the house—and split the money. I'm sure the house is worth a fortune."

"Granny," said Joanna, now almost squirming with discomfort, "Why are we talking about this now? I mean, you look like you've got quite a few years left in you."

"You're right, of course," said Louisa, softening again. "Why spoil this little time we've had together?"

"Exactly," said Joanna.

Feeling that the conversation, and the brandy, had now produced the desired effect, Louisa asked if Joanna would mind if she excused herself and turned in for the night. Although it was still relatively early, and Joanna was feeling highly stimulated by the events of the day, she told Louisa that she too was tired.

"Well," said Louisa, knowing that Joanna was just being polite, "I told Harris to put a television set in your room and—there are books all over the house, and—dare I say it—there's always the piano."

As she said this, a thought occurred to her.

"D'you know what I think? I think that wicked old Harris probably left the ballroom doors open on purpose. He said something earlier about how you were always playing that piano when you were a child."

"Don't be upset with him," said Joanna.

"Upset?" said Louisa. "I think I'll give him a raise."

As she rose to leave, Louisa walked over and seated herself next to Joanna and took her hand. "Thank you, dear," she said, "for not hating me when you had every right to, and for caring enough to try to understand me."

"Of course," said Joanna, "and thank you, too."

"D'you know what I think we should do?" said Louisa, suddenly sounding almost girlish, "I think we should go shopping tomorrow and buy you some clothes."

"Oh, that would be great," said Joanna, "but—"

"No buts," said Louisa, "and, of course, we'll arrange to get you some spending money as well."

"Oh, no, Granny," said Joanna, "That's too much."

"My dear, the wolf isn't exactly knocking at the door," said Louisa. "Not just yet."

What Joanna didn't know was that, for a woman like her grandmother, anything less than a perennial overabundance of cash reserves was regarded as an impending financial crisis. While the news she had received earlier in the day from her financial advisors suggested that it might be advisable temporarily to tighten her belt a notch—there were still many, many more notches to go.

"I'm planning to look for work as soon as I can," said Joanna, "I'll pay you back as soon as possible."

"You'll do no such thing," said Louisa. "It'll give me such pleasure to be useful to someone. To be useful to *you*, that is. Oh, dear, I *am* tired."

This time, it was Louisa who embraced Joanna.

"I'm glad you're here, my dear," she said as she rose to leave. "Sleep well."

"You too, Granny," said Joanna.

—6—

Looking around the library after Louisa went to bed, Joanna came across an illustrated book about the House of Worth, which she stayed up reading until the wee hours—and, as a result—she awoke much later than usual the next morning.

As she was about to head downstairs in search of breakfast, she heard the sound of a vacuum cleaner coming from what had been her grandfather's room. Realizing that she had never caught more than a fleeting glimpse of his room, she walked to the open doorway and peeked in, startling the uniformed maid who was cleaning the room.

"Good morning, Miss," said the maid, in a musical Irish brogue. "Is there something I can do for you?"

"Oh, no," said Joanna. "I'm sorry. This is—this *was*—my grandfather's room, and I've never—I mean, I haven't seen it for a long time. I'm sorry to disturb you."

"Not at all, Miss," said the maid.

It struck Joanna as odd that her grandfather's room, which was presumably unoccupied, should be getting cleaned when there was so much else to be done—but as she was about to move away from the door, the maid asked if it would be alright to clean the Blue Room, and she felt guilty for having had the thought. Heading back toward the stairs, she noticed that the door to her grandmother's room was slightly ajar, and poked her head in to say hello to Louisa, who was sitting up in bed, reading the Wall Street Journal.

"I'm glad I'm not the only one who sleeps late around here," said Joanna.

"Oh, I've been up for hours," said Louisa, "I get up with the chickens. But I was feeling a little lightheaded this morning—and that fussy old Harris ordered me back to bed.

You know what tyrants butlers are. Or, perhaps you don't. But come in, my dear. I've been waiting to speak with you. I'm afraid we'll have to postpone our little shopping spree."

"Oh, that's okay," said Joanna. "I have a few clothes with me. I'll be fine as long as there's a washing machine."

"Yes, well, that's what I wanted to talk to you about. Sit down, Joanna."

Joanna sat on the side of the bed, making an effort to hide her concern—which Louisa was nevertheless able to detect.

"I'm fine, dear," she said, patting Joanna's hand. "That's not what I wanted to talk to you about." Then, reaching for an envelope that was lying on a bedside table and handing it to Joanna, she said "I've made out a check for you. I want you to have this."

Joanna stared at the envelope but didn't open it until Louisa, like a child on Christmas morning, said "Well, go on. Open it!"

Inside the envelope, folded into a piece of Louisa's stationary, was a check for $50,000.

"Oh, my god! Granny!" said Joanna, when she could catch her breath. "You must be kidding. I can't take this."

"Now, you listen to me, young lady," said Louisa, "writing that check made me feel better than anything I've done in a very long time."

"But Granny, I can't," said Joanna. "I mean, you just told me you were having financial problems."

"Oh, problems, yes," said Louisa, dismissing for the moment her own inflated concerns on the subject. "Anyway, who knows if I'll even live long enough for it to matter?"

Joanna was about to interrupt her, but Louisa stopped her.

"Look," she said, "I realize that that may seem like a great deal of money to you, Joanna, but it's not much more than a month's worth of taxes and upkeep on this house. In fact, if I weren't such a sentimental old fool, I'd sell this house tomorrow and be a very rich woman again."

"But, Granny, this is—this is *too* generous," said Joanna. "I just can't."

"I don't want to hear another word about it." said Louisa. "Are you really going to deny me the one pleasure I've had within recent memory?"

"Well," said Joanna, "I guess if you put it that way—but I feel like I'm being blackmailed."

"Call me old-fashioned, but don't blackmailers normally *take* money?"

"Emotional blackmail," said Joanna. "You know what I mean."

"Well, that's settled then," said Louisa. "And, if it makes you feel any better, there's a catch."

"Aha!" said Joanna.

"Yes," said Louisa. "When you go shopping, you have to buy at least one dress."

"Something very conservative, I assume?"

"Let's just say something classic, shall we? Oh, and there's one other thing."

"What's that?"

"I want you to promise to play a bit of Chopin for me now and then."

"I think that can be arranged," said Joanna, now fighting back tears, which Louisa nipped in the bud.

"Good," she said, "Now off you go, and have a lovely time. After you've had your breakfast, ask Harris to give you the keys to the convertible. It's a beautiful day to have the top down."

Louisa told her that the convertible, which she had named Scarlett, was nearly ten years old, and hadn't been getting nearly enough exercise recently. Joanna said that she had never even been in a convertible, let alone driven one—and that she found the prospect very exciting.

"Well then," said Louisa, "I strongly suggest—now, I don't want you to think I'm a controlling sort of person—but I *strongly* suggest that you turn left onto Bellevue and drive all the way to the end—after which you must turn right, then take the first left, and have a spin along the coastline. And if *that* doesn't make you feel like Grace Kelly, there's no hope for you."

"That sounds wonderful," said Joanna. "but would Grace Kelly be wearing jeans?"

"Oh, use your imagination," said Louisa, "Or go shopping first. Must I think of *everything*?"

"Right," said Joanna. "I think I understand the assignment here. You want me to try to locate my inner heiress."

"Yes, something like that" said Louisa, lowering her eyelids in a playfully condescending way. "Now run along before it clouds over and the whole thing is moot."

"Alright then, I'm off," said Joanna—feeling, for the first time in years—an uncomplicated and unthreatening sense of excitement. Grabbing Louisa's hand as she was about to leave, she said, "Granny—I can never thank you enough."

"Oh, go on," said Louisa, only half pretending to deflect what was, in fact, an immensely gratifying response.

When she was halfway out the door, Joanna turned back and asked, "By the way, did you ever meet Grace Kelly?"

"Yes, but that's a story for another day. Now go!" she said, blowing a kiss.

Driving Louisa's bright red convertible out onto Bellevue Avenue, Joanna's already high spirits were lifted even higher—so much so that she didn't recognize the jogger she almost hit when entering the road. Hearing him yell "Hey you!" as she sped away, she assumed she was being reprimanded–so she waved an arm in the air and yelled "Sorry! I couldn't see you because of the wall" over her shoulder.

Pace Hamilton, who was the jogger, stopped in his tracks. Being a connoisseur of cars, he couldn't help noticing the fact that Joanna had just driven out of a Bellevue Avenue mansion in a Rolls-Royce Phantom Drophead Coupé. He'd recently seen a new model of the same car with a sticker price of over half a million dollars, and he reckoned the car Joanna was driving to be worth at least half that amount.

"Playing piano in a dive bar, eh?" he thought–and, joking to himself that he was clearly working in the wrong bar–he resumed his jog.

As Louisa had said, it was indeed a beautiful day. The midday sun was casting a perfect glow on both sides of the avenue and, owing to the fact that it was lunchtime on a weekday, and still several weeks from peak season, there was virtually no traffic to take Joanna's attention away from the topographical, botanical, and architectural delights that came into view at every turn.

After a spin around the coastline, she drove to the Newport Casino, where she found a secluded table facing the grass tennis lawn, and where she had the most delicious clam chowder and lobster salad she had ever tasted. When it came time to pay the check, she used a credit card that hadn't been used in such a long time that she was compelled to identify herself over the phone. After that, it occurred to her that perhaps she ought to visit Louisa's bank and open an account. As the process unfolded, she felt almost as though she were depositing stolen money, until she reminded herself that her guilt sprang from a much deeper source than any sum of money could have produced. Apropos, as she was leaving the bank, it occurred to her that it might behoove her to spend some of that money on a good psychotherapist.

As the late afternoon began to advance toward sunset, she found a public parking lot near the wharves that line that part of the bay. As she strolled along Bowen's Wharf and Bannister's Wharf in a state of blissful fatigue, a few tourists were gathering for drinks in the more picturesque watering holes—and for the first time in months, she truly craved a gin and tonic. Walking across Queen Anne Square to the park that abuts Trinity Church, she found a bench and called William to bring him up to date on the overnight developments in her living situation—as well as her unexpected urge to drink. William pointed out—or rather reminded her—that the kind of drinking urge she was having was to be expected, and that the overnight change in her living situation was a perfect confirmation of the day-at-a-time philosophy on which AA is based. He also suggested that it might not be a bad idea for her to attend a meeting as soon as possible.

Joanna sat in the park for an indeterminate amount of time, with her thoughts roving, retaining all of the fatigue of the day but not too much of the bliss, until sunset was underway—suggesting that it might be time for her to head home. The very fact that she had used the word "home" as a part of that thought process was cause for considerable gratitude for the day she'd just had—and it wasn't until she was driving into the courtyard of Windstone that she realized she had never gone shopping.

—7—

Passing the library door, Joanna saw Harris making preparations for dinner, and stopped to say hello and ask about her grandmother. He seemed very pleased to see her—addressing her now as Miss Joanna. That morning, when handing her the keys to the convertible, he had floated "Miss Cushing," but a polite shake of her head suggested to him that this was no better than plain "Miss," and so he decided to try "Miss Joanna," which he considered a viable compromise, and which also pleased Joanna (mainly because she was amused by the archaic sound of it). He said Mrs. Livingston appeared to be feeling better than she had felt earlier in the day, and that he expected her downstairs presently. Not having gone shopping, Joanna figured there wasn't much point in heading upstairs to dress for dinner, and chose instead to visit the ballroom, the doors to which were once again open. Leaving the doors open and seating herself at the piano, she began playing Chopin's Ballade No. 2.

Presently, as Harris had predicted, Louisa was in the doorway, but this time she walked straight to the piano, and this time Joanna did not stop playing until there was a natural break in the music. The section that followed was much too difficult for her to play without having practiced, but the first section comes to such a quiet, logical conclusion that Louisa was none the wiser.

"It sounds like a hymn," said Louisa.

"It does, doesn't it?" said Joanna. "I never thought of that. You know—that's interesting."

"What's interesting?"

"Well, the next part of it sounds kind of diabolical. I wonder if Chopin meant to juxtapose the sacred and the profane."

"What a wonderful mind you have, Joanna."

"I must have inherited it from you."

"Alright, that's enough of that. Anymore of that and Harris will come rushing in with a firehose."

"Oh, he can't be as mean as that," said Joanna.

"Mean? He's an absolute marshmallow. But he likes to maintain the illusion. You know, the intimidating English butler."

"That's his job, isn't it?"

"With Harris, it's more like a calling. In any case, I wouldn't take away his illusion of authority for the world."

"They don't make them like Harris anymore," said Joanna.

"They don't even try," said Louisa.

"Granny—it's really none of my business, but—you have made arrangements for his retirement, haven't you?"

"Knowing Harris, I'd be surprised if he hasn't saved every penny he's ever earned. But yes, after our talk last night, I called my lawyer to discuss the arrangements for both of you. I think I'll leave you the house, by the way."

"If only you could leave me Harris to go with it," said Joanna, who then caught herself. "Oh, that sounded awful, didn't it?"

"That's your Livingston blood coming out," Louisa said with a mixture of pride and sarcasm.

"Ugh," was all that Joanna could say.

"Careful there, young lady—I'm still a Livingston. Actually, I'm more of a Winthrop but, either way, I'm still your grandmother."

"Damn," said Joanna, "I thought we were becoming girlfriends."

"Yes, well, there are limits—even with girlfriends. In fact, *especially* with girlfriends."

"Would you like a brandy?" Joanna asked.

"Oh, very diplomatic, my dear. You'd have made a good hostess. I think Harris has made a gin and tonic for me and—well, something for you. Let's go have our drinks and talk about life."

"Sounds good," said Joanna, "but since you get to have all of the alcohol, do I get to do most of the talking?"

"Oh, dear me," said Louisa, "You really *are* a Livingston."

As the two women settled into the library with their drinks, Harris asked is there would be anything else before he went off to fetch dinner. Louisa thanked him, and said there was nothing she could think of, whereupon he did his usual "Very Good, Madam" with a respectful nod of the head, and made his exit. Louisa stared at the doorway for a moment after he'd left, and then turned to Joanna.

"As if there's anything I could think of that he hadn't thought of already," she said.

"Do you know anything about his past?" Joanna asked.

Louisa hesitated for a moment. She knew much more than she was prepared to say—even to Joanna—knowing how much Harris cherished his privacy.

"Not much," she said. "I know he came from a coal mining town—poor lamb. Somewhere in Yorkshire, I believe. Absolutely ghastly. Coal mining, that is, not Yorkshire. Yorkshire's beautiful."

"He seems kind of depressed," said Joanna.

"Wouldn't *you* be? If you'd left some coal mining village to seek your fortune, only to find yourself chained to a lonely old woman—*and* still having to work as hard as a coal-miner?"

"Do you have any idea how hard coal miners work?" Joanna asked.

"Not really," said Louisa with some chagrin, "but I'm sure it's very, very hard."

"How long has he worked for you?"

"Hmm—I think he came about five or six years before you were born, however long that might be," said Louisa, with a wink that acknowledged an unspoken moratorium on the topic of age. "Of course, he used to have a large staff."

Joanna saw another opening for what might be a delicate subject. "Granny—what happened to your other houses?"

"Oh," said Louisa, making an effort to sound blasé, "The one in Palm Beach had to be sold—probably so that we could afford to keep this one—and the one in New York, we donated to a school. I believe there was some tax advantage involved in that one. I've never been good with money. Your grandfather always took care of everything."

"Hmm," said Joanna, not elaborating until her grandmother requested her to do so.

"Well," she said, "it sounds like—maybe you were living beyond your means."

"I have been known to do that," said Louisa with a guilty smile.

"So, maybe—"

"Maybe what?" said Louisa, suddenly defensive.

"Maybe Grandpa wasn't as good at managing money as you thought."

"As I said—you're a real Livingston."

"Oh, Granny, I'm sorry. I didn't mean to hurt your feelings."

"Oh, it's alright," said Louisa. "I'm all for the naked truth. I just don't like hearing it from others."

"I hear that," said Joanna, as they both laughed.

As it happened, the naked truth, of which Louisa was entirely unaware, was that Seth Livingston had had a serious gambling addiction, and had more than once risked his share of the income from the Livingston family's real estate empire, particularly during their annual visits to Monte Carlo.

The arrival of dinner created a pause in the conversation, but after Harris had poured Louisa's wine and left the room, the conversation continued—now that they were capable of eating and talking simultaneously.

"I did try to find you, you know," said Louisa.

To Joanna, the remark seemed to come out of left field, but she didn't yet know to what lengths her grandmother was willing to go to steer away from certain topics.

"You did?" said Joanna. "How? On the Internet?"

"On the what?" said Louisa, not hearing the word clearly.

"Don't tell me you went old-school and hired a private detective or something," said Joanna.

"Alright," said Louisa, "I won't tell you that."

"Oh, no! Did you really?"

"Well, of course I did! Wouldn't you?"

"Obviously not!" said Joanna. "God, I feel so guilty. I mean—that you went to all that trouble."

"You mustn't feel bad. Hiring a detective was just my way of trying to control everything—as usual." Then, remembering her breeding in the nick of time, she added, "And of course I was concerned for your welfare."

"God! Now I feel as if I should pay you back for the detective too."

"If you say one more word about money, I will go to my room," said Louisa. "Although, I guess I'm supposed to send *you* to your room."

That's right. You're the parental figure here."

"Unfortunately, I'm a bit out of practice. Although, maybe that's a good thing. It never was my strong suit."

"Okay, no more of *that*. And, I promise—no more talk about money. So—what else should we talk about?"

"Well," said Louisa, drawing the word out to about three syllables, "we could always talk about men. For heaven's sake—do you realize that—here we are, two women who've been talking for two days, and we haven't brought up the subject of men once."

"Oh my god! I should call the Guinness Book of Records," said Joanna.

"The what?" said Louisa.

"The Guinness—oh never mind. But, you do know what the Internet is, don't you?

"Of course I do," said Louisa. "What do you take me for? But never mind all that. *Is* there a man your life?"

"Oh, we're back there, are we?" Joanna said ruefully. "Um—no. I mean, definitely no! Definitely not."

Louisa was concerned by the adamancy of Joanna's response.

"You're not still—a tomboy—are you?"

"No, granny, I'm not a lesbian, if that's what you mean. Although sometimes I wish I were. Anyway, there's no man in my life at the moment. But—I did meet a cute bartender last night. He was even intelligent. And nice."

"A bartender? Is that wise?"

"It's just a job, Granny. I think he wants to be a writer."

"That's even worse!" said Louisa, which made Joanna laugh but made Louisa start to cry.

"Oh, no! What's the matter?"

"Nothing, for a change," said Louisa. "I'm just happy."

Joanna was so touched by this that it made her antsy enough to want to change the subject—even if it meant talking about men. "You know," she said, "we *have* talked about men. We've talked about Harris."

"Yes, well, he doesn't count," said Louisa.

"Granny!" said Joanna.

"Oh, for heaven's sake, that's not what I meant! Really! You're incorrigible. I meant to say that Harris is much more than a man."

"Amen to that," said Joanna.

"And now," said Louisa, stifling a yawn and leaving most of her food untouched, "I think I really will go to my room. You don't mind amusing yourself for the rest of the evening, do you?"

"No, of course not," said Joanna, hiding her concern at Louisa's sudden bouts of fatigue. "But—let's do something together soon. How about if we go out to dinner and a movie?"

"That sounds lovely," said Louisa. "Are there any Cary Grant pictures playing?"

"I don't think so, but you know what? Let's just rent a movie."

"It's a date," said Louisa.

"Good night, Granny."

"Good night, darling."

Although she was tempted to rummage through the library again, Joanna chose instead to pursue a different pastime. She took off her shoes, put her feet up, sat very still, took a few deep breaths, and allowed her mind to wander. This was always her favorite thing to do when she was high, but she'd recently discovered it to be equally interesting when she was sober. When she was high, her thoughts always tended to go to the same places—but when she was sober, they were much less predictable—and it was thus that she now found herself thinking about her grandmother, and trying to imagine what Louisa Livingston would have been like as a young woman. The idea that the subject even interested her made her smile. It was that smile that comes when one's spirit is in a place one never expected it to be, accompanied by the knowledge that this is the place where one's spirit needs to be.

PART TWO

8

Throughout the summer of 1948, the newspapers had been full of what they called the Winthrop-Livingston nuptials and, as the wedding day approached, the coverage was reaching a fever pitch. In the year that a new fad called television was about to be launched, when you included the foreign language papers, there were upwards of forty newspapers in New York City alone, and competition was fierce. Every detail that journalists could glean from the families, friends, and employees of the betrothed couple—as well as a number of details that were gleaned from the tawdry imaginations of some of the reporters themselves—had found their way into print. From the fluctuating number of carats in the engagement ring to the more or less accurate guest list, no real or imagined detail was too trivial to be "of interest to our readers." In 1948, the public still clamored for news about high society almost as much as they clamored for news about movie stars. After all, the luminaries of high society—and debutantes in particular—had been, so to speak, the original movie stars.

The major news stories of that year, apart from the murder of Mahatma Gandhi and the Soviet blockade of West Berlin, had been largely uplifting. Israel had been declared a state, the Western European Treaty had been signed, a thirteen-year-old girl with a liver condition named Sylvia Beckingham had become the first patient of England's revolutionary new National Health Service—and the debut of the Polaroid Land Camera was about to facilitate a giant step toward the concept of instant gratification. With the Second World War safely behind them, and the baby boom having been detonated—with a lot of help in the form of cheerleading from Hollywood—America was basking in the glow of something greater than mere peace and prosperity. The country was feeling optimism on an unprecedented scale. And, other than the birth of a child, nothing inspires more optimism than a wedding.

As the mid-September date approached, the families and guests of the betrothed couple were returning to New York from their summers in Rhode Island, Maine, the South of France, and the English countryside—and everyone was excited about the big wedding. Everyone, that is, except the bride, who was also the only major figure involved in the wedding who had not yet returned to New York.

Young Louisa Winthrop was the eighteen-year-old daughter of Reggie Winthrop and his estranged wife Lila. Reggie was what was then known as an international playboy, and Lila had been dubbed "the original flapper" by a fickle press who'd forgotten having previously bestowed that title on Zelda Fitzgerald—who, after many years in asylums and out of the headlines, had just died tragically—and tragically unnoticed. Whether together or apart, Lila and Reggie were always good for a scoop or a headline; so it followed as a matter of course that the wedding of their only child would provide ample fodder for the gossip columns and the society pages. And, for the more serious-minded, the positions of prominence held by various members of the groom's family in the worlds of business and politics lent a reassuring ballast to the proceedings. All in all, it was just as well that the wary bride-to-be had cloistered herself in her grandmother's house in Newport—far away from all the hubbub.

In fact, it was no longer her grandmother's house, because Letitia Winthrop had recently given the house to the young couple as a wedding present. When Louisa balked that it was much too generous for a wedding gift, her grandmother told her that, in truth, the trip to Newport was becoming far too taxing—after which she boarded a transatlantic ocean liner, followed by the boat train to London, then a train from London to Dover, followed by an all-day channel ferry to connect with a French train, after which she motored to her villa in Eze-sur-Mer, which was only a few minutes further drive from the excitement of Monte Carlo—*none* of which Tish Winthrop found too taxing.

In deference to the proud Livingstons, Louisa had offered to change the name of the house from Winthrop Hall to Livingston Hall—but her fiancé had suggested what he felt was a clever compromise by combining the two names into the name Winston—which Louisa disliked because it sounded like a person's name. Given that the property faced the open sea and was made of stone, Louisa suggested adding a letter to each of the truncated names—and thus the name Windstone was born. Seth suggested the further compromise of Windstone Hall, but Louisa said it already sounded "a trifle too Brontë-esque without adding back the Hall," after which Seth suggested the name Windstone House—which, to Louisa, sounded like an inventory ("wind, stone, house: 1 each," she said derisively). In the end, Seth came up with the name Windstone Place, which he felt had a soothingly English countryside appeal to it. Louisa thought it was a tepid compromise, but she didn't say so, because she knew that everyone would inevitably use the shorthand of Windstone—which meant that she could have her way while making Seth believe he had gotten his.

And so, the bride-to-be found herself alone in a newly christened, very big house with only a skeletal staff—the caretaker and his wife—remaining after the season. Being down for the count (as she called it), her primary distraction, other than reading, was the redecoration of her favorite guest room, which she was now calling the Blue Room, because she had chosen to furnish it all in blue—or as much blue as her exacting taste would permit. It was her intent to make the room a nursery, when the need for one arose, and she had convinced herself, based on something she'd read about the power of suggestion, that by filling the room with blue, she would give birth to a boy. The world, she decided, was not as well-suited for girls—even privileged girls like herself—as it was for boys.

That summer, she had begun to give herself a ballet barre every morning in the ballroom. Her best friend and soon-to-be maid of honor, Gloria Milford, had recommended a handsome young Italian pianist, Mr. Amato, who came to play Chopin for Louisa while she did her morning barre—which got slightly longer every day. *Anything* to take her mind off the wedding. Or so she told herself.

Louisa wasn't exactly dreading the wedding and the subsequent marriage, but she wasn't exactly looking forward to it either. It had been more or less arranged by the two families. The prospective groom, with Princeton behind him and a promising career in the family business ahead of him, was all for it, but Louisa would have preferred to study for a few more years. Her friends were just starting at Wellesley, Barnard, Bryn Mawr and Vassar—and even though they all envied her such a brilliant marriage—she envied them more.

Still, whenever they were together, she liked Seth Livingston well enough. He was good-looking and charming and, unlike most of the eligible young men in her set, made an effort to appreciate her wit and encourage her curiosity. To her family, however (although they would never have admitted it), an alliance with the Livingstons was something of a coup, particularly considering that the Livingstons seemed willing to overlook Lila and Reggie's shenanigans.

For more generations than anyone could remember, the Livingstons had enjoyed an impeccable position in Society. Not only was their vast wealth derived primarily from the ultra-respectable source of real estate (never mind that the Iroquois had been "persuaded" into parting with that real estate so that it could be granted to the original Livingston patroon in the 17th century), but the Livingstons had since married into every distinguished family in New England and, more recently, into European nobility. The onetime queen of New York and Newport society, Caroline Astor, when asked to define the benchmark that allowed new blood to enter into society, had said that it took about three generations for the money "to cool off," and the Winthrop fortune—originally derived from a nationwide chain of 5 and 10 cent stores—was just now three generations old.

But none of that mattered to Louisa, because Louisa found the Livingstons dull. Yes, they were highly cultivated and read all the right books. Yes, they made interesting references and allusions, always couched in irreproachable grammar—even with occasional flashes of wit—but despite all of that (although *that* was what made them bearable), there was something stultifying in their detached temperament and their unapproachable hauteur. There was no soul behind any of them. Louisa would find herself almost drifting off during conversations with her future in-laws. To her few close friends, she had begun calling them the Living Stones.

And now, to complicate matters further, there was the beautiful young Mr. Amato, with his beautiful hands, playing his beautiful Chopin every morning. And although barely a word had been exchanged between Louisa and Mr. Amato, a volume of unspoken words had passed between them. Louisa had only recently discovered, thanks to Gloria, that his first name was Antonio—and the two of them had taken to calling him AA whenever anyone else was present. Italians, at the time, like the Irish, were not considered acceptable in fashionable society. In Rhode Island, an Italian name, unless it was associated with the Florentine Renaissance, was associated with gardening, bricklaying or stonemasonry. Young Mr. Amato's grandfather, in fact, had been brought over from Italy along with a group of expert stonemasons for the sole purpose of constructing the mansions of the Gilded Age like the one in which he now found himself playing the piano.

Despite having what her social set called a certain *je ne sais quoi*, Louisa Winthrop was aware that she was not conventionally beautiful—but when Mr. Amato smiled at her, she felt as if she became beautiful. She wanted to believe that this had something to do with Mr. Amato's Italian taste and sensibility. It didn't occur to her that Mr. Amato was two generations removed from Italy and had never even visited there. The only detail of his past that Gloria Milford had been certain about (or somewhat certain about), was that his people came from Rome, which, as Gloria pointed out, was the original quarry—*even before France*—of classicism and good taste. But in Louisa's fanciful imagination, Mr. Amato needed to come from somewhere even more romantic than Rome. Florence perhaps—or maybe Verona.

From time to time, in the mirrors that covered most of the ballroom, she'd seen what she thought was a seductive look on Mr. Amato's face. The first time she had met her fiancé was in that very ballroom, where she had ventured a witticism that hadn't quite landed. Bess of Hardwick was one of the women in history Louisa most admired, and recalling the famous phrase "Hardwick Hall—more glass than wall," she'd made up a parody about there being "a *ball* at Winthrop *Hall,* in a room quite *tall*—more mirror than *wall.*" Seth's polite yet vacant smile telegraphed the dubious success of her little jest, but he was amused after she explained it. Of course, thought Louisa,

Mr. Amato wouldn't know about Bess of Hardwick either. But he knew about Chopin—which meant he must also know about George Sand. But why, she asked herself, was she even thinking such thoughts when she was about to be married to another man? Surely it was just cold feet. Or maybe she just had too much time on her hands. In any case, that's the way she explained the situation to Gloria Milford—whose response was to fold her arms, raise her eyebrows, inhale dramatically through her nose, and blink her eyes once in very slow motion. After that, as much as she trusted Gloria, Louisa decided that any further thoughts concerning Mr. Amato should be kept to herself.

After her ballet barres, Mr. Amato always rose reluctantly from the piano, shook her hand courteously and bowed slightly from the waist. One day—not long after the day she'd laid her case before Gloria Milford—he brought her hand to his mouth and gave it a gentle kiss. It made her feel like a princess. A guilty princess, but a princess nonetheless. After that, she thought of Mr. Amato for the rest of the day and the evening. She kept meaning to call him to explain that her schedule was becoming far too busy, and that she'd better postpone the ballet barres to some future date. At one point, she got as far as lifting the receiver off the telephone, but she reminded herself of her wedding dress, and the beautiful trousseau she'd bought in Paris in the spring. After all, ballet was such an excellent form of exercise, and she would naturally want to stay fit for the wedding—and, of course, the honeymoon.

The next morning, for the first time, Mr. Amato arrived late, ready to extend a profound apology.

"Miss Winthrop—" he said breathlessly.

"Louisa, Mr. Amato," she said, also breathlessly.

"Antonio," said Mr. Amato.

There was no ballet barre that morning.

—*9*—

Several weeks after Joanna's arrival at Windstone, Harris was arriving at the top of the stairs early one morning, when he heard unexpected sounds coming from the Blue Room. As he was about to knock, the door was suddenly flung open—and there stood Joanna, dressed for jogging.

"Joanna!" said Harris, before he could catch himself, his face turning crimson.

"Well, well, well," said Joanna teasingly, "aren't we familiar this morning?"

"I'm so sorry," said Harris. "I meant to say Miss Joanna, of course, but—"

"Oh, Harris. You really are too funny with the butler shtick sometimes," she said. "You could call me Jo-Jo for all I care. Anyway, it's not as if you recognized me, right? I mean—out of bed at 7:00 a.m. *and* dressed to go jogging?"

Harris appeared considerably relieved, and Joanna wondered to herself how it was possible that this man, who was so evidently beloved by her grandmother, should forever go to such pains to avoid a professional misstep of any kind—which in turn caused her to reflect on her own struggles with self-esteem, bringing that unwelcome line of speculation to an abrupt end. As she began almost bouncing down the stairs, Harris did his throat clearing thing and asked if he might say something.

Joanna stopped, turned around, and said "Absolutely. I'm all ears."

"May I just say," Harris began, formally but with undoubted sincerity, "It's been a great pleasure having you in this house these past several weeks."

Joanna was determined not to become emotional at what she considered an ungodly hour of the morning, especially considering that she was in such an untypically buoyant and ambitious mood. Instead, she merely took his arm and said, "Harris—as my Granny would say—you really are a treasure."

"Thank you, Miss," said Harris, biting his lip.

Joanna resumed her spirited descent down the stairs, talking to Harris over her shoulder.

"I'm sure by the time I get back you'll have feudal order restored to the house, but (here she stopped and turned around again) you really are a good egg." As she was about to take another step, she turned around yet again and added "Oh, speaking of eggs—I think I'll skip breakfast today."

As she passed the open library door, she saw Louisa, who was already fully groomed and reading. Almost skipping into the room, she kissed Louisa on the forehead.

"Who are you?" asked Louisa, "And what have you done with my granddaughter?"

"I know, right? You've never seen me this perky this early in the day."

"I've never seen you this perky *or* this early in the day," said Louisa, "but I choose to believe it's a good omen."

Joanna shrugged, blew another kiss toward her grandmother, and headed out to jog. As she was leaving the courtyard, absentmindedly donning her headphones before reaching the curb, she ran into a fellow jogger who, based on the impact, seemed to be a powerful man.

"Sorry" she said, and was about to move past him, when he grabbed her arm from behind—which, though gently done, both shocked and annoyed her.

"Look!" she said vehemently, as she turned around, "I said I was sorry, but—*Oh*, It's you! Wait a minute...wait a minute..."

"Pace," he said dejectedly. "Pace Hamilton."

"Right," she said. "I knew it was something unusual. And you had a funny nickname, too. Was it—Porky?"

"You have an intimidating sense of humor," said Pace.

"Only because I'm massively insecure," said Joanna.

"About me?" said Pace, incredulous.

"About anything," said Joanna. "So you can stop fishing."

"Whoa!" he said. "Busted again. Right off the bat, just like last time."

"Yeah, I know," said Joanna. "Remind me again why I'm single? Oh, right. Anyway, I told you we'd run into each other."

"I didn't realize you meant it literally," he said.

"I love a man who knows how to use the word literally," she said.

"Literally?" he said, attempting a crafty smile.

"Quit while you're ahead, my friend," she said.

"Yeah, let's move on," he said, "Literally. Do you wanna jog together?"

"Um—I don't really want to jog at all. I just woke up with an excess of energy for the first time since—well—ever—but it seems to be evaporating already."

"Have you had coffee?" asked Pace.

"I have not."

"Shall we?" he asked.

"Yes, please. My treat. Let me just go and grab some cash."

"No, no, it's on me." said Pace.

"But I still owe you a meal. Remember?"

"Oh, *I* remember," he said, with a little more slickness in the sound than he would have chosen if he could have done a retake. "We'll get around to that."

Gesturing with the grandeur of a French courtier, with a slight bend of the waist and a tilt of his head, with what Joanna would come to cherish as his dorky playfulness, Pace indicated the direction of the waterfront, and they were off.

It was a beautiful morning in the peak of the summer tourist season. At this hour of the day, however, the tourists would be having breakfast in the countless hotels, inns, and B&Bs around the island, and therefore the streets were still relatively calm. At Pace's suggestion, Joanna took a seat on a bench in Trinity Park, in order "to bask in the beauty of the morning," while he walked across the lawn to Starbucks. A few minutes later, he emerged with two large coffees and a large paper bag.

"Oh my God—drugs!" said Joanna, as he handed her a coffee. "Thank you so much." Then, as he opened the paper bag with a flourish to produce a large, luscious looking pastry, she added, "Be still my heart. I think I'm in love."

"Is that all it took?" he asked.

"Oh, you can stay too, if you like" she said.

"Ouch," said Pace.

"Just kidding!" she said, "*Obviously*. But you do walk right into them."

"You're too fast for me," he said.

"Well," she said, "don't worry. Coffee and sugar will slow me down."

"So," she continued, taking a bite of the pastry, "you're a writer?"

"Yeah—ostensibly" he said, with a more pronounced look of diffidence than Joanna had yet observed in him.

"Well, that proves it!" she said, offering him a bite of the pastry. "I mean, who else uses the word ostensibly these days?"

"Yeah, I guess so," he said, still in the same defeatist tone. "And you? You play the piano, right?"

This was an attempt to sound detached about someone who had become almost an obsession for him. He had so wanted to see Joanna again that he had taken to jogging around the walls of Windstone every morning for the past several weeks, in the hopes of bringing about this very coincidence.

"Wow," she said. "I forgot that it could sound so mundane. But, yes—I play piano."

"Oh, mundane, eh?" he said. "Now, that's just as fancy as ostensibly, don't you think?"

"Nah," she said. "I don't think any word with two syllables or less could really be called fancy."

"Oh, no?" he said, "Give me a minute. How about—no, wait—how about—errant? Two syllables. Totally fancy."

"Errant," she said. "Bravo. Well done." For a moment, they drank their coffees in silence, and then she added, "What a couple of dorks we are."

"Yeah, well, at least for a *couple* of dorks. Have you ever been the only dork in the room?"

"Um—yes," she said, trying to sound cool about being very uncool. "Like—when they leave you alone in a corner and say they wish they hadn't wasted good drugs on you?" Then, seeing his bemused expression, she said, "Wait—that's not what you meant, is it?"

"No," he said. "I'm talking about being such a dork that you're not even invited into a room where anybody has drugs. I never really liked drugs anyway. Did you?"

"Um—l'il bit," said Joanna—after which, perceiving a look of discomfort on his face—she made a deft U-turn in the direction the conversation was heading. "So," she said, "tell me about writing. I mean—tell me about your life."

"You know," he said, "funny you should ask. I think I'm about to have a life."

Sensing Pace's reluctance to continue to talk about himself, Joanna gently goaded him into what she called spilling the beans.

"Well—um—so," he began, tentatively, "the thing is—I'm always trying to write *something* and—I'm always coming up with what I think are great ideas but—for some reason—I never finish any of them."

"Oh, that," said Joanna.

"You do that, too?"

"Yes, but we're talking about you."

"Oh—right," he said. "So—the thing is—a while back—after graduation—to celebrate graduation actually—I spent a couple of years sailing around the world with a couple of friends."

"Really? That sounds amazing! So, have you written a book about it?"

"Well, no," said Pace, "not exactly. But I kept journals the whole time—I mean every detail."

He took a deep breath, stopped stumbling, and blurted out the rest.

"So, I've written a long article about it that's intended to be the first in a series and I just sold it to a sailing magazine. The whole series! How cool is that?"

"Very cool! Of course, now you'll have to finish it."

"Yeah, there's that. But, I kinda have no choice about that, since they already paid me for it. For one thing, my dad would kill me."

"Well, we can't have that!"

"No, we can't have that."

For a moment, with his unfamiliar eagerness to talk about himself being temporarily depleted, Pace seemed to study Joanna.

"You're really pretty, by the way," he said.

"Oh, thanks," she said, "So are you. By the way."

They were now both feeling the awkwardness that masks the underlying excitement of such moments. Joanna, who was something of a virtuoso when it came to transitioning away from awkward moments, was the first to break the silence.

"Hey! You know what? I think we should do something to celebrate your success."

"Totally," said Pace, overjoyed at any suggestion that would allow him to spend more time with her. "Got any ideas?"

"I dunno," said Joanna playfully, "We could—go sailing?"

"Twist my arm, why don't you," said Pace. "I'm *so* up for that. Should we go home and change clothes or just go for it? My boat's like—a ten minute walk from here."

"I say we just go for it," said Joanna. "Anyway, my sailor suit's at the cleaners."

This made Pace laugh, albeit somewhat nervously, and as they prepared their trash for recycling and got up to leave, he turned to Joanna with a somewhat more serious look on his face.

"That *was* a joke, right?" he asked.

"Yes, Pace," she said, "that was a joke."

—10—

The Great New England Hurricane of 1938 was the most destructive hurricane ever to make landfall in the recorded history of New England. Starting harmlessly off the coast of Africa on September 9, and gaining strength on its westward and then northward path, the storm made landfall in Rhode Island eleven days later.

In 1938, warnings about hurricanes were often a last-minute affair, and the warning that had ultimately been issued (which greatly underestimated the storm's intensity) was too little too late. When the storm finally made landfall in Rhode Island in the late afternoon of September 21st—having already taken a mighty toll on Long Island—the loss of life and property was tremendous. The storm surge that swept up Narragansett Bay left much of downtown Providence under thirteen feet of water. People drowned in their cars and school buses. Old-timers in Rhode Island still spoke often about the storm. Only a couple of nights earlier, during a thunderstorm, Louisa had been telling Joanna horror stories about the '38 hurricane. The least tragic story (but certainly not the least interesting) was about how one of Louisa and Joanna's favorite actresses, Katharine Hepburn, had narrowly escaped death while attempting to wade to safety from her family's beach house down the coastline in Old Saybrook. Virtually all of her personal belongings, including her 1932 Oscar, were either lost or destroyed—although the Oscar was eventually found.

Today, on this radiant summer morning, as she and Pace powered out into the bay, the water, due to a near total lack of wind, was almost as smooth as glass—but Joanna found herself thinking about the '38 hurricane. Nor could she help thinking about her parents sailing out into a comparatively minor storm—never to return. In an attempt to dispel those thoughts from her mind, she began to focus instead on feeling guilty about suggesting a sail on a day that was not an auspicious one for the sport. Except when she was under the influence—and rarely even then—Joanna could never allow herself the pleasure of undiluted happiness for any appreciable amount of time.

Somewhere in the trajectory of her mood swing, Pace handed Joanna a large pair of binoculars. Looking through them, one of the first sights she noticed was an immense French Renaissance château whose sloping grounds extended to the water's edge. It reminded her of the châteaux of the Loire Valley she'd visited as a child, and she asked Pace if he knew anything about it. He responded with an embarrassed shrug—but told her with some excitement that, after they sailed past the mouth of the bay, he looked forward to showing her what had once been the summer home of Edith Wharton. Joanna expressed surprise at his keen interest in Edith Wharton, until he reminded her of his college major. He told her that, for a period of time, Wharton had been his favorite female writer, and that *The Age of Innocence* was his favorite book. He said his copy of the book had become so dog-eared and highlighted that his mother had bought him a Kindle so that he might make notes electronically and find his favorite quotes in a flash.

As they neared the point where the lee of the land would cease to be an inhibiting factor, Joanna maneuvered and secured the lines in a way that suggested a considerable degree of familiarity with the sport of sailing—and once having passed the lee—the raised sails billowed with that exhilarating snapping sound Joanna had not heard for many years. There was a reason why the America's Cup Race was held at the mouth of Narragansett Bay for over fifty years—predictable winds—even on a calm day such as this.

Following a childhood habit, once they were underway, Joanna made her way forward and stood in the bow pulpit, allowing the sun, wind, and spray to work their magic. But even then—in what had once been her favorite place on a boat—she began thinking of Leonardo DiCaprio and Kate Winslet in the same position on the Titanic, which, to a degree, dampened her excitement. On her way aft a few minutes later, she stopped to double check the jib halyard before rejoining Pace, who was steering.

"Something tells me this is not your first time on a sailboat," said Pace.

"I've been sailing since I was five. I'm a Rhode Island girl, remember?"

"Wow," he said.

"What?" she asked.

"A girl who's smart and funny and pretty and who loves sailing. What more could I ask for?"

"Yeah—if only you liked shooting heroin, we'd be a perfect match." Seeing more of a look of concern than the simple laugh she'd been expecting, she quickly added "I'm kidding! I've never shot heroin of my life. Yet."

But the moment had come.

"Joanna," Pace said hesitantly, "Is there something you'd like to tell me about drugs and alcohol?"

"Why, yes, father. I was wondering when we were going to have this conversation."

"Aw, jeez! Did it really sound that pompous?"

"Kind of—but that's ok. It makes for a light segue into a serious topic."

"So—you *do* have a problem with drugs and alcohol?"

"Wow. You sure like cutting to the chase," she said. "It's a good thing you don't write suspense novels."

“Oh, I’m sorry,” he said, “did you have a big dramatic scene planned?”

“I beg your pardon!” Joanna said this with a playful, clearly faked indignation, behind which she was actually relieved to see that Pace could show a bit of backbone.

“I’m just getting you back,” he said, smiling.

The seemingly uncomplicated aura of safety in his smile made Joanna feel that she could be honest with him about anything—forgetting the fact that she had often had cause to regret arriving at that same conclusion with other men in the past.

“Right,” she said, “So—the thing is—I *do* have a history of addiction.”

She waited for a reaction that didn’t come.

“Do you still want to get to know me?” she asked.

“Of course I do! I mean—it’s all in the past, right?”

“Well, that’s the thing. I’m not sure if it’s ever *really* in the past. But you’re safe for the moment. We’re on a boat.”

“Oh,” he said ominously, “Don’t go below.”

“Oh, no!” she said, “Fully stocked bar?”

“Fully stocked bar.”

“Ooh, you know what? We could get wasted together.”

“Sure,” he said, after giving it a moment’s consideration, “But I think we should take the boat in first.”

“Pace!” she said, almost tempted to wag a finger at him. “I was kidding.”

“I knew you were kidding,” he said defensively.

“You did not. You were totally weighing the possibilities in your mind.”

“Whoa! Busted again,” he said. “Okay—I *was* weighing the possibilities—but I also knew you were joking.”

“Trust me,” she said, “the last place I would ever want to get wasted is on a sailboat. If you only knew—”

Here she stopped herself, trying once again to blot out any thoughts about her parents.

"I'm sorry," she said. "We don't even know each other. Why am I telling you all about my sordid past?"

"Why not?" he said. "It's nothing to be ashamed of. You sure do apologize a lot."

"I know," she said. "Sorry about that."

Once again, she felt it was imperative to change the subject. As they had walked to the marina, she had mentioned that she was living with her grandmother.

"You know, my grandmother wanted to be a writer."

"Oh yeah? Did she ever write anything?"

"She wrote a novel, but I guess it wasn't very good. Seems to run in the family."

"What does that mean?"

"Oh, nothing," she said—and as she did, a sadness came over her like a cloud blotting out the sun. It was the look that often accompanies the words "Oh, nothing." It reminded Pace of one of his favorite highlighted passages from *The Age of Innocence*, when the enamored Newland Archer looks into the sad eyes of the young Countess Olenska as she struggles to come to terms with what others consider her scandalous past:

"It frightened him to think what must have gone into the making of her eyes."

Pace took her hand and drew her a little closer to him, at which point a sudden movement of the boat threw her against him.

"Well, thank you, Neptune," he said.

"Um—don't write any romance novels either," she said. "A line like that could be a deal-breaker."

"Yeah," he said, "that was pretty bad." They both attempted to laugh, at which point he decided to kiss her, after which she smiled and put her head on his chest.

"You know," he said, "if I'm gonna be schooled, I'm glad it's by you."

Suddenly, Joanna pulled away from him.

"Oh my God!" she said. "What day is it?"

"Wednesday," said Pace. "Why? Do you not kiss on Wednesdays?"

"Oh, shit!" she said, ignoring his response. "I'm such a fuckup!"

Being at sea in more than just the literal sense, Pace wasn't sure what to say next.

"I'm confused," he said. "What just happened here?"

"I have a job interview today," said Joanna, still pretty much yelling, "Right about *now*, in fact. With a *school*!" She said the word school in such a pointed way that Pace looked completely confused by it.

"You said you'd been schooled!" she said.

"Oh, right," he said, now feeling he understood the situation. "So, what should we do?"

"I cannot believe I fucked this up. For some reason, I thought today was Tuesday, and I even did a dry run of getting up early! I mean—there's like—maybe three schools in this town that could hire a music teacher, and I got an interview with one of them, and I'm going to miss my fucking appointment. I'm sorry about the language, but—"

"No problem," he said. "I mean—what better place to curse like a sailor, right?"

"Don't even," she said.

"Right," he said, unaware of how irritating it was of him to continue to maintain a modicum of levity, "No comic novels either, I guess."

When she didn't react, he began to fully register the degree of her hurt and concern, He hugged her in a way that she could only half return, and said the only words she wanted to hear at that moment.

"Ok, let's take her in."

Except for what was necessary for navigational purposes, very little was said as they sailed back into the harbor and secured the boat to its mooring. The battery on Joanna's phone was nearly dead, so she had decided earlier to turn it off until she could be sure of a steady signal. After the boat was moored, she turned her phone on and saw that she had a new voice message.

"It's probably the school, wondering where the hell I am," she said.

Instead, it was from Harris, telling her that her grandmother had taken a rather bad fall not long after Joanna had left that morning.

—11—

Forgetting for the moment about the school, Joanna called the house, and Harris answered almost immediately. He said he hoped he hadn't disturbed her. He said Mrs. Livingston had been adamant that her granddaughter shouldn't be bothered with this, but added that he felt she would want to know.

"Of course I would want to know," said Joanna. "Is she okay?"

"I believe she will be, Miss. The doctor is with her now"

"Thank goodness you were there."

"Indeed, Miss." (For the moment, neither of them noticed that he had resumed calling her "Miss.")

"Look—I'm not very far away," said Joanna. "I was just out sailing with a friend, and I was heading home anyway, so—I'll be there as soon as I can."

"Is there anything I can do for you in the meantime, Miss?"

"For me?" said Joanna. "Heck no! Just take care of her. I'll be there as soon as I can."

"Very good, Miss."

"Pace!" she said, almost startling him with her sudden burst of energy. "I'm sorry. My grandmother's had an accident. She hasn't been feeling well lately and it sounds like she had a bad fall. Anyway, I have to go now."

"Of course," he said, wondering whether a kiss on the cheek or a friendly hug would be the most appropriate parting gesture at this point.

"Um—do you want me to come with you? In case she needs anything? Or maybe just for moral support?"

"No, that's okay," she said, "I mean—yeah, sure. Actually, that would be great. And—I'm really sorry about that outburst on the boat. It had nothing to do with you, obviously. I was just angry with myself. As usual."

"It's totally fine," he said. "I understand."

"God," she said, "You're too good to be true. Anyway, we'd better get going."

As they hurried through the front door of Windstone a few minutes later, Harris was coming down the stairs.

"Harris!" said Joanna, "We got here as fast as we could. How is she?"

"I believe she's better, Miss. The doctor has just left, and she's sitting up in bed and seems to be in good spirits. She's very keen to see you."

"Okay, I'll head upstairs. Oh, this is my friend Pace, by the way."

"How do you do, sir?" said Harris.

"Nice to meet you," said Pace. "Is there anything I can do?"

"Does she need anything?" asked Joanna.

"Yes, Miss. She'd like to have the chair behind the desk in the library. I was just on my way to fetch it."

"I can do that," said Pace. "Just show me where it is."

"Oh, sir, I couldn't ask you to do that. It's quite heavy."

"Just show him where it is," said Joanna. "I'm sure you have enough to do."

"Very well," said Harris. "It's this way, sir."

"Do you know anything more about what happened?" asked Joanna, as she followed the two men into the library.

"As far as I was able to determine, it seems Mrs. Livingston fainted and hit her head."

"So—you didn't see it happen?"

"No, Miss. I was passing by her room, and I heard her moaning."

"God, that must have been scary," said Joanna, as Pace began moving a large chair from behind the desk.

"Whoa!" said Pace. "Where're we going with this?"

"Just to the top of the stairs, sir. May I help you with that?"

"Stairs, huh? Yeah, maybe I could use some help. Why don't you go ahead, Joanna."

"Okay, sure," she said. "But you guys be careful. We don't need anyone else getting hurt today," at which point she hurried up the stairs, knocked on her grandmother's door, and entered without waiting for a response. Louisa was sitting up in bed with a large bandage on her forehead.

"Granny!" said Joanna, "You naughty girl! What have you been up to?" Then, crossing to the bed, she said. "Are you okay?"

"Of course I am! What an old woman Harris is—making such a fuss."

"Excuse me. You're the old woman here. Harris was just doing his job—above and beyond as usual."

Louisa was busy apologizing and agreeing with Joanna, when Harris and Pace entered the room carrying the chair.

"Oh, my goodness," she said, looking at Pace, "who is *that*?"

"Where shall we put it, madam?" Harris asked.

"Oh, by the fireplace, I suppose. Just move that chaise out of the way."

"Oh, Granny," said Joanna, moving away from the bed to where Pace was standing, "This is my friend Pace."

"Pace Hamilton, ma'am," said Pace. "It's nice to meet you."

"Pace Hamilton? You're not Hammy's son, are you?"

"I am," said Pace.

"Well, no wonder you're so good-looking. I knew your father when he was your age. Come to think of it, I knew your grandfather when he was your age."

"Small town," said Pace under his breath to Joanna, in response to an inquisitive look from her.

"Yeah, right," she said back to him.

"I didn't realize you knew my granddaughter," said Louisa, "but then, she's very secretive."

"That's not true," said Joanna. "I'm an open book."

"Well, well, well," said Louisa generally, and then, repeating it to Joanna specifically, "Well—well—well."

"Unfortunately, Granny, Pace has to be going," Joanna said, knowing exactly how ridiculous she sounded.

"Oh, no—surely not!" said Louisa.

"I don't have to be going," said Pace.

"Yes you do!" said Joanna, squeezing his hand very gently. "Remember that thing you had to do?"

"Oh, right," he said. "That thing."

"Oh, for heaven's sake!" said Louisa. "For the first time in years a handsome man turns up in my bedroom—no offense, Harris—and you want to throw him out?"

"Pay no attention to her," Joanna whispered to Pace. "She's just had a head injury"

"I heard that!" said Louisa.

"You *would* hear *that*, wouldn't you?" said Joanna.

Pace wasn't really following the gist of the conversation, but he was clear about the idea that it was time for him to excuse himself.

"It was a pleasure to meet you ma'am," he said. "I hope to see you again soon."

"Feel free to drop in anytime," said Louisa. "And you needn't be with Joanna."

"Granny!" said Joanna.

"What?" said Louisa, with great innocence. "I was just being courteous to your young man."

"Yes of course you were," said Joanna, turning to Pace. "Well, say goodbye to everybody."

"Goodbye, ma'am. Goodbye, Harris."

"Goodbye, sir."

"Goodbye, Pace," said Louisa. "I hope to see more of you."

"Sounds good to me, ma'am."

"Yeah, right, buh-bye everybody," said Joanna, as she hustled Pace out of the room.

As the two of them stood at the landing atop the stairs, Pace sensed that he should let her speak first.

"Okay, that was embarrassing," she said.

"Why?" he said. "She seems adorable."

"Is that what you call that?"

"I can't believe she knew my grandfather."

"Oh, she knew everybody. She probably knew Attila the Hun."

"I don't understand why you're so upset."

"Well, because—for starters—I was kind of freaking out about her. I thought she was much worse off than she seems to be. And then, I missed my job interview, and I—I don't know what to do next."

"So—why don't you let me go call the school and explain what happened—and you go and take care of your grandmother?"

"Yeah, that sounds good," said Joanna, wearily.

"At least I have a legitimate excuse for a change," she said. "Oh, it's, uh, Thames Street Elementary School. It's in my phone."

"And where's your phone?"

"It's on the desk in the library, but the battery's about to die, so you might want to use the house phone—which is also on the desk." She started to return to her grandmother's bedside, but stopped to add "Thanks for everything, Pace. And congratulations again."

"Oh, sure, thanks. Um—see you soon?"

"Sure. That'd be great. Leave your number next to my phone and I'll text you mine."

"You got it. See ya."

"See ya."

Re-entering Louisa's room (as Harris was leaving in order to mop away his perspiration in private), Joanna walked to the side of Louisa's bed and placed her hands on her hips in a mock reproachful manner.

"Well, well, well!" said Louisa. "Pace Hamilton the Third."

"The third for *you*, apparently," said Joanna.

"Well—well—well."

"Stop saying well, well, well."

"I can't think of anything else to say."

"That's because there isn't anything else to say."

"Oh, but there is. How could you be going out with Pace Hamilton and not tell me about it?"

"Because I'm not going out with Pace Hamilton. I barely know him."

"Harris says you were out sailing with him earlier. That sounds like going out to me."

"You were right. Harris is an old woman."

"Now, that's not fair. After the doctor left, I asked him if he knew where you were, and he said you'd been out sailing with a friend."

"You're right. Sorry."

"I know I shouldn't tease you, dear, but I'm just so happy for you, that's all."

"There's nothing to be happy about."

"Oh, well. I suppose we'll just have to wait and see how it turns out."

"Yes, I suppose we will. At least until our first date."

"He seems very fond of you already. You should see the way he looks at you."

"I've seen the way he looks at me."

"I really don't mean to pry—but aren't you excited?"

"Yes you do mean to pry, and yes maybe I'm a little excited, but I can't afford to feel excited about men right now. I'm too vulnerable. And anyway, I'm not used to things going well with men."

"Oh, my dear, I'm so sorry. You're very serious about this, and I'm behaving like the village matchmaker. Why don't we talk about it? That is, if you want to."

"We *are* talking about it," said Joanna, seating herself on the side of the bed. "I mean, there really isn't anything to talk about. I wasn't kidding when I said I barely know him. Today was, like, the second time I've ever seen him—and both times were by accident."

"Oh, I see," said Louisa, trying not to look disappointed.

"I mean, he seems nice. Almost too nice. And here I was thinking he was just some cute bartender who wanted to be a writer—but there's something about the way you said Pace Hamilton the Third that makes me think there's more here than meets the eye."

"Well, what meets the eye is good enough," said Louisa. "But really Joanna—you don't know about the Hamiltons?"

"No, but I'll bet you're going to tell me about them."

"Certainly not. Not unless you want me to."

"Oh, go for it. You're chomping at the bit."

Louisa drew herself up as much as the setting allowed.

"I'll thank you to remember that I'm a lady and not a lady's maid," she said.

"Whatever! Come on. Spill the beans. I'm all ears."

"I'm waiting for you to run out of metaphors," said Louisa.

Joanna smirked playfully at Louisa and gave her the kind of beckoning gesture that says "Let' go. Get on with it," and Louisa took the cue as readily as if she were an actress about to play her big scene.

"*Well!* What can I say? I mean—*the Hamiltons*—Hammy and Caroline. She's one of the Barclays, you know."

"No, I don't know."

"One of *the* Barclays," Louisa said, undaunted. "My dear, they're legendary. One of those old families who've lost most of their money, but manage to produce the most beautiful daughters—who just happen to end up—surprise—marrying the richest men in the world." Then, seeming to inhale for the first time, she added, "My dear, the Barclays are the epitome."

"So, what you're saying is—Pace is rich."

"Rich? His father is worth at least a hundred million."

"A hundred million? Then why is he working as a bartender?"

"Oh, they all do that nowadays," said Louisa. "At least for a while. It's some sort of work ethic thing. And why not? Keeps them off the streets. Did you happen to notice a great French chateau on the water's edge as you were sailing out today?"

"How could you miss it?"

"Yes, well, I think that's the point of it—but, in any case, that's Hammy and Caroline's place. It's called Hamilton Court."

"Really?"

"I know—it sounds a bit grasping to me, too. I would have just called it Water's Edge, or something like that. Anyway—*that* is your young man's summer cottage."

"He's not my young man."

"Yes, well, something has to be done about that."

"How hard did you hit your head earlier?"

"Very funny. But you're the one who needs to be hit on the head."

"Alright—now you really are behaving like the village matchmaker."

"I know, but isn't it fun? You know, when I saw the two of you together, it just—looked right somehow."

"To you."

"Oh, now. You must be somewhat fond of him."

"Granny, I've only seen him twice."

"Well, you'd better get a move on then, hadn't you?"

"I think I need to go to my room."

"Oh, how tiresome of you. Please don't say you're going to take one of your naps."

"It's a bit early for a nap, But I'll think of something. You, on the other hand, should definitely get some rest. And stay away from the Jane Austen novels."

"Very funny. I'll have you know I've decided to get back to work on my memoirs. That's why I wanted that chair."

"Your memoirs? Really? How exciting."

"Yes, I just came across them today. Maybe that's why I fainted. I really must change the name, though."

"Oh, what's it called?" asked Joanna, with genuine enthusiasm.

"*Before the Sunset Fades*," said Louisa.

"Oh, dear," said Joanna, who was such a terrible liar at such moments that she'd long since given it up.

"Exactly," said Louisa. "Who did I think I was—the Vicereine of India?"

"I think it sounds more like Madame de Maintenon," said Joanna, trying not to giggle.

"Oh, that's cruel," said Louisa, "although—I'm terribly impressed that you know who that is. But, darling, I need you to help me update the title."

Without even appearing to think, Joanna said "How about *After the Ball*?"

"Oh, how perfect! Although, at this point, I might have to call it *Better Late Than Never*."

"Ooh, I like that, too," said Joanna, taking Louisa's hand at the sudden reminder of her mortality. Louisa had recently turned eighty-six; but she was still such a force that, until today, her actual age had seemed to hold little significance for those around her.

"Now look," she said, "don't wear yourself out or get too excited about those memoirs right now. You really should rest."

"I will. I promise," said Louisa, at which point Joanna got up and kissed her on the forehead and said "I love you."

Louisa grabbed her by the arm.

"What did you say?"

"I said I love you."

"Oh, Joanna, I can't remember the last time anyone said that to me. I love you too, dear. And I'm proud of you—no matter what you decide—you know, about being Mrs. Hamilton."

"Thank you," said Joanna, trying to laugh it off. "Now, seriously, get some rest."

"I will. I promise."

Meanwhile, downstairs in the library, Pace had been writing out his phone number when a text message appeared on Joanna's phone. It was from someone named Danny, and it read:

hey babe im tired of sleeping alone so get over yourself and come home alright? xxx

"It figures," he said out loud as he was about to leave. There was a moment when he thought about crumpling up the note with his phone number written on it, but then he remembered there was an ex-boyfriend, and changed his mind. He had felt a bit dismissed a few minutes earlier, but then he reminded himself that he barely knew Joanna, and that she was upstairs dealing with a sick grandparent.

—12—

Antonio Amato may have been born and raised in America, but in some ways he was very much a Roman. Accordingly, despite the fact that, in 1948, merely holding hands with a girl like Louisa Winthrop implied a certain level of commitment—and strictly honorable intentions—he did not hesitate, now that they were on a first name basis, to grab hold of her and kiss her in a way that she had never been kissed. When she could pry herself from his vicelike grip, she raised a hand with the intention of slapping his face, but chose instead to use both of her hands to grab hold of his face and kiss him back—as *he* had never been kissed. Antonio's Corsican mother had taught him to be wary of aggressive, or even autonomous women. She dreamed of a daughter-in-law from a Norman Rockwell painting; but Antonio allowed himself to dream without pre-conceived ideas. His mother's dreams arose from her worldview—whereas his worldview arose from his dreams.

To say that this romantic interlude suddenly rocked the foundations of Louisa's world would be an understatement. In a heartbeat—in a skipped heartbeat—everything that Louisa had felt was lacking in Seth Livingston was embodied by the young man with whom she was locked in this ongoing embrace in the ballroom at Windstone—and it was some time before the ether subsided long enough for her to fully realize her dilemma. Feeling that she might be on the verge of screaming, she pulled away from him and ran upstairs to the Blue Room, locking the door behind her.

Preferring not to dwell on her predicament, she almost wished that Antonio would follow her up the stairs and break down the door, if only to distract her. Instead, after a few minutes had passed, he arrived quietly at the door, against which she was leaning on the other side, and whispered "Louisa" in such an ethereal way that she immediately unlocked the door and threw herself into his arms.

There was no bed in the room as yet—but then, if beds were a prerequisite to the consummation of love, the human race would have ceased to exist a long time ago.

Barely a week remained before Louisa would have to leave for New York, and she and Antonio spent every hour together that they could arrange without arousing the suspicion of the caretaker and his wife. When they told each other their life stories, as lovers do, Louisa told him that she had grown up wanting to be a ballerina, at which point he removed her shoes and kissed her "beautiful feet."

A few days later, he told her he had planned a big surprise for her. It was a parting gift, but he couldn't bring himself to call it that. After taking an early bus to Providence, they proceeded to take the short train trip to Boston. It was Antonio's first time in Boston, and since he had told her that the surprise was coming later in the evening, she showed him the few sights with which she was familiar. Later, they had an early dinner, and Louisa had her first taste of Italian food and chianti. After the dinner, she said "Thank you. This was a lovely surprise."

"This wasn't the surprise," he said, beaming like a schoolboy, after which he shuffled her into a waiting taxi and took her to a theatre where a visiting foreign ballet company was presenting Tchaikovsky's Sleeping Beauty. Earlier in the day, he had arranged with a local cousin of his who had purchased the tickets to leave them with the owner of the restaurant—and the owner had surreptitiously given them to Antonio on his way to the men's room.

Louisa had seen many ballets, but she had never seen The Sleeping Beauty, and she was as thrilled by the prospect as Antonio had hoped she would be. The seats were not located in the section of the theatre she was accustomed to, and yet she couldn't have been happier. From the fierce opening of the overture to the languid strains of the wedding pas de deux in the third act, Louisa loved every minute of it, and she chose to believe that when Antonio reached for her hand at just the right moments, it meant that he had learned something of the art of ballet from watching her in the ballroom. If she had had to pick a favorite moment, though, it would have been the Rose Adagio in Act I, when the young Princess Aurora has come of age and is beseeched by young suitors, each handing her a rose from which she inhales the scent before tossing them gaily aside—the better to dance with the young men who brought them.

Roses were Louisa's favorite flower, and Rose was her middle name, which she had always preferred to Louisa. In fact, among her closest friends, she was called Rose. She had even asked her beloved granny to call her Rose, but the best the old woman could do was to call her Louisa Rose—which was perhaps even better. Antonio, on the other hand, called her Rosa, which made her go weak in the knees. During an intermission, Louisa caught him staring at her, as he tended to do. She offered him a penny for his thoughts (although they were perfectly obvious free of charge), and he said "Tu sei la mia bella rosa." Louisa spoke French well enough to figure out his Italian, but she asked for a translation anyway. "You are my beautiful rose," he said—and she nearly fainted. That night they stayed in an inexpensive hotel, which was the only time Louisa had any serious qualms about what she had now begun to think of as a pre-nuptial-extra-marital-affair.

Returning to Newport the following afternoon was a very melancholy sequel to their carefree day away in Boston. Her departure for New York was now becoming imperative, and was more a matter of hours than days away. Every fiber of Antonio's being compelled him to beg her to stay—to stay forever—and she waited for him to ask, determined that she would say yes if he did.

Antonio was twenty-two, four years older than Louisa, which was not enough to lay claim to any great difference in life experience, but he'd had twenty-two years of life experience of a certain kind. He knew all too well what a struggle life could be when striving to survive financially became the paramount concern—and it was obvious from all his talks with Louisa that she had no idea what any of that could, and almost certainly would, be like. She had been born and raised at too high an altitude to be able to see that.

Antonio had no driving ambition in the world except to be happy. He was content to play the piano, and to teach the piano when possible, which left him ample time to be a human being rather than a human doing. Louisa had made it clear that she cherished him because he was so many things Seth was not. He loved music, not because his family had always had a box at the opera and the symphony, but for its own intrinsic merits. He visited museums, not because his family donated sizable sums of money and even priceless works of art to them, but because that was where they kept the art. He loved books, not because they made his conversation cleverer or more trenchant, but because books spoke to his spirit and made him feel less alone in the world.

All of that Louisa could relate to, and it was because of all of that that she told herself she loved him. But Antonio knew, from everything she had told him, that Seth Livingston was good and kind and generous and respectful of her interests and indulgent of her whims—*and* he had something Antonio would never have—a vast fortune derived from New York real estate. Indeed, since the death of John Jacob Astor exactly one hundred years earlier, the Livingstons had gradually assumed his mantle as "New York's landlord," and that source of revenue wasn't ever likely to dry up.

—13—

Much to the annoyance of both families, Louisa delayed her arrival for nearly two full days longer than the absolute latest she had promised. Her mother Lila was becoming borderline frantic. To the consternation of the publicity-shy Livingstons, Lila and Reggie had been making themselves as available to the press as their sporadic sense of decorum would allow, and they had run out of excuses for their daughter's continued absence. They'd even patched over their former differences enough to enjoy an occasional cocktail hour together.

"Who does she think she is—Greta Garbo?" Lila shouted at Reggie one evening after a few rounds of martinis. This made Reggie laugh, which pleased and annoyed Lila in equal measure. Lila and Reggie had been great fans of Garbo during the thirties, and had once had a laugh about how long and with what a buildup Garbo's entrance in a film was often held back—presumably to increase the anticipation of it.

"It's not funny," said Lila, though she was now laughing herself.

"Well," said Reggie, drunk enough to speak his mind, "If I were marrying into that mausoleum I'd have cold feet too."

"Did you just say something clever?" asked Lila, who was also beginning to feel the effects of the martinis.

That was the kind of remark, depending on how much fuel they'd both imbibed, that might have led to a huge fight during their marriage. But they had since reached a point where they could appreciate each other's way of communicating without personalizing every word. Indeed, if this conversation had taken place during their marriage, Reggie would probably, about now, be telling the indignant Lila that she didn't really give a hang about the wedding, and that she only wanted Louisa to be present for the added publicity.

As the cocktail hour crossed over into its second hour, Lila's phone rang, and shortly thereafter a butler cleared his throat in the doorway and informed Mrs. Winthrop that Mrs. Winthrop was on the telephone. Letitia Winthrop was calling to tell her daughter-in-law that *her* daughter had finally arrived from Newport.

Lila asked her mother-in-law to put Louisa on the phone, but Letitia said that Louisa wished to speak to no one for the rest of the evening—but promised to be available for any and all last-minute arrangements and rehearsals that required her presence starting early the next morning. Before Lila could completely lose her temper, the older Mrs. Winthrop told her that she would be better off to relax and stop making such a fuss. Except when she was traveling or entertaining—which was most of the time—Tish Winthrop never liked a fuss.

While all of this was taking place on Fifth Avenue, a couple of blocks away, on Park Avenue, young Seth Livingston was attempting to alleviate the concerns of his ultra-conservative family regarding some of the glitzier aspects of the proceedings thus far—stressing over and over again that it was, after all, 1948. What he didn't tell them was that even he was greatly relieved by the arrival of the bride. He'd barely even acknowledged to himself just how worried he'd become in the past few days.

Nonetheless, despite the various anxieties of all concerned, the wedding went off that weekend "without a hitch"—as Tish Winthrop had assured everyone one it would—always adding "no pun intended." The bride's family had originally suggested the ultra-fashionable St. Thomas Episcopal Church on Fifth Avenue and 53rd Street—but with regard to the location, the Livingstons were implacable. Livingston family weddings, they said, had been held at Grace Church for generations. This meant trekking down to Broadway and 10th Street, something about which Lila was "not terribly keen." It was a gloomy, cramped old place in her view—but Reggie pointed out that its smaller size meant fewer invitations, which made the wedding even more exclusive than it already was. Reading from one of the newspaper accounts of the wedding arrangements, he came across a famous quote about Grace Church from Matthew Hale Smith, who had written "To be married or buried within its walls has been ever considered the height of felicity."

A begrudgingly acquiescent "Mmm" was the only response Lila could be bothered to express on the subject.

When the day finally came, it was one of those slightly too warm September days, and every eligible High-Brahmin WASP in New England had somehow been stuffed into the nave of Grace Church. There was also a crowd of reporters and onlookers gathered outside the church, whom those inside the church insisted were responsible for the collective body heat of the occasion. For her part, the only people Louisa was happy to see were her bridesmaids, particularly Gloria Milford, Millicent Sloane, and Daisy Delafield. They were her only intimate friends, and though she longed to tell them all about Antonio, she realized it would be utter madness under the circumstances.

Indeed, facing Seth was the hardest part. Even if Antonio Amato had never existed, gazing at Seth with the proper mixture of demureness and adoration during the ceremony would have been tricky enough for a girl like Louisa, but (as she reminded herself pretty much every minute) Antonio Amato *did* exist. Therefore, her attempts to look demure came off more like reluctance, and her looks of adoration resembled the goggle-eyed vacuity of a dead fish. Fortunately, only the priest and the groom were able to see her facial expressions during the critical portions of the ceremony. The priest was too busy to take notice, while Seth wrote it off to the sort of stage-fright brides were said to experience, and decided therefore it should be taken as a compliment.

Similarly, later that night, he concluded that her resistance and discomfort in response to his attempts at physical intimacy were no more than what was to be expected from a young, inexperienced female.

—14—

Joanna left Louisa's room with the intention of spending some time reading in her own room, but she passed by the Blue Room and walked downstairs to the library. The brilliant afternoon sunlight was streaming through the library windows, most of which faced directly west onto Bellevue Avenue. At first, she sat quietly, absorbing the peace and beauty that surrounded her. For the past eighteen years, she had lived first in a college dorm, then in a tiny cramped apartment that she avoided as much as possible, followed by Danny's apartment, which was in the noisiest part of town. While at college, like so many other college students, she had convinced herself that being a college student was the reason she "partied" as much as she did. After college, it was the daily effort to avoid her bleak and unorganized little one-room apartment that was the reason she gave herself for being out every night at a bar, often not returning home at all. Then, of course, Danny became the reason for her accelerating abuse of drugs and alcohol.

With regard to Danny, who'd initially been an enabler and a provider, this was partly true. But by the time she eventually became aware that she "might have a problem"—after Danny had reversed course and was trying to get her to stop—she was convinced that her problems with drinking and drugging were the result of her life choices—and not, as was the case, the other way around.

From childhood through adolescence, her grandparents' library at Windstone had never been a particularly alluring room for Joanna, especially since she had all the books she needed in her own room upstairs. But now, along with the ballroom and the Blue Room, it felt like a sanctuary. After a few minutes' reflection on all the things she had to be grateful for, she walked around the room, looking out of the two windows that faced west, and then through the French door that faced south and opened onto a continuation of the herbaceous border. There was nothing in any direction that didn't contribute to a sense of comfort and safety—until her phone vibrated on the desk. It was the text message from Danny, which might have brought back the long-gone knot in her stomach if she hadn't simultaneously noticed the two notes that had been left by Pace.

One of the notes read "The school says it's no problem. Just call them to re-schedule," under which he'd drawn a smiley face. The other note contained his name and phone number, which brought a smile to her face.

Looking around the room, her attention was drawn, for the first time since Louisa had shown it to her, to the photo of her great-grandmother Lila, and she walked over to look at it. Next to the photo of Lila was a photo of the Duke and Duchess of Windsor—and behind that was a beautiful photo of Grace Kelly, thanking Louisa for her hospitality during a visit to Windstone.

"A story for another day," she said, replacing the photo of Kelly and picking up the one of her great-grandmother. She wondered what she might have thought of Lila if they had known each other. From everything she'd heard, Joanna guessed that she would have had very little in common with Lila Winthrop—apart from genealogy and alcohol—and the same, no doubt, applied to Reginald Winthrop.

Reggie's mother Tish, however, sounded like a fascinating character—and it suddenly struck Joanna that all five generations of them had lived a significant part of their lives in this house—indeed in this very room. Such a glaringly obvious fact, she thought, and yet somehow, she couldn't quite visualize anyone actually living at Windstone other than Louisa and Harris.

In fact, it was only recently that she'd been more or less compelled to think about her family history at all. A few weeks earlier, she had begun seeing a therapist. She would have preferred to find a woman therapist, but William had strongly recommended his own therapist, who was a man—and a man in his late fifties at that. Reluctantly, but out of courtesy to William, she decided to give the man a try—and she was very glad that she had done so. His maturity and his life experience were obvious assets, but she was more impressed by the youthfulness of his spirit, which was more ebullient than her own. More often than not, it seemed to her as if she were speaking with a contemporary—albeit a contemporary who was much more pulled together than herself. He had told her at the outset that he specialized in the treatment of addiction, but what he didn't tell her was that he was a recovering alcoholic himself. Having sunk to the depths of homelessness, crime and eventual imprisonment in his mid-twenties, he had begun his recovery and education while in prison, and had recently celebrated thirty years of sobriety.

His name was Derek Churchill, and between his impressive sounding name and the effortless suavity of his appearance and manner, Joanna assumed that he was most likely a descendant of the local gentry—or rather the seasonal gentry—whereas, in actual fact, he was the offspring of a poor white trash family from New Hampshire. This may have been the reason that one of Derek's go-to pieces of advice was the maxim "Appearances are deceiving," which he knew to be axiomatic in general, as well as having specific application to himself.

Because she chose her friends according to mutual interests and similar world views, Joanna had always had a few gay male friends. Furthermore, she found that she was drawn to gay men because she enjoyed having male company, but without the usual subtext. A gay male friend could tell her she was looking lovely without an ulterior agenda. Alas, as she once told Derek, she had never learned how to find the kind of women friends who could fulfill that same function, and she found it incredible that the woman who came closest to fulfilling that function—with the possible exception of her new friend Pamela, who'd been her roommate at rehab—turned out to be her own grandmother.

Derek had a way of saying things that would land squarely on the mother-lode of Joanna's vulnerabilities. One day, she was telling him that she felt very guilty about her grandmother paying for psychotherapy, especially since people like Louisa Livingston regarded therapy as something akin to voodoo.

"Do you have a hard time accepting generosity?" Derek asked her, already knowing the answer.

"Um—usually," said Joanna. "There always seem to be strings attached."

"If there are strings attached, then it's not generosity," he said. "There is such a thing as altruism, you know—although, I'll grant you, it's pretty rare."

"Yeah, I hear you," she said. "I'm sure there are no strings attached when it comes to my Granny, though. That's why I feel guilty."

"That's why you feel guilty—but that's not why you feel guilty," he said. Initially, this sounded enigmatic to the point of being oracular—after which it made her very anxious, because she understood it completely. In the absence of alcohol and drugs, Joanna had two default responses for dealing with anxiety: she would either make a joke or she would become flirtatious. She knew that jokes didn't work well with Derek, so she went with flirtatious—or rather a blend of the two.

"What if I said I had guilty thoughts about you?" she said.

He was momentarily flattered, but this was familiar territory for Derek, and he recognized the behavior for what it was. He'd also known her long enough by that point to be able to share something personal about himself.

"You do know I'm gay, don't you?" he said.

"Oh, no," she said, feeling embarrassed but also disappointed in what she considered to be her infallible gaydar, "I didn't know that."

"More relevantly, though," he added, "I'm your therapist."

"That's awesome," she said, "I mean, that you're gay," immediately wishing she'd said something that sounded just slightly more grownup.

Despite awkward moments like that, seeing Derek was turning out to be one of the best decisions of her life. Little by little, Joanna learned that literally nothing she could say could shock Derek nor induce him to judge her—and the more she became aware of that, the more she was able to push the envelope. The same was true of her relationship to William and—to the extent she was able to read them—of the people at her AA meetings.

Life had turned into something good for her—not just something to be endured, as it had too often been in the past. Things had been so good, in fact, that she had fallen out of the habit of going to regular meetings, for which both William and Derek had gently but unequivocally admonished her. She had even planned to go to a meeting that very evening with Pamela, but then her grandmother had had the accident, and she now felt that she should stay close to home.

Looking through the bookshelves, she came across a copy of *The Age of Innocence*, which both Pace and Louisa had highly recommended. Joanna remembered liking the film version very much, and decided to give the book a try—but realized that she was too sleepy to focus on a book that surely merited her full attention. For one thing, she'd gotten up earlier than usual in order to jog (for which she was still dressed), and then the sail had happened. She'd forgotten that something about gulping in sea air while expending the energy necessary to the maneuvers of a small sailboat can lead to a pleasantly soporific effect. As she was looking through the books, Harris stopped in to offer her some of the tea sandwiches that he was preparing to serve to her grandmother. It suddenly occurred to her that she hadn't eaten, and the food was not only welcome, but made her feel even sleepier. She took down the volume on the House of Worth in order to flip through the lovely photos again. A few pages into it, she dozed off.

A long time after that, judging by the dwindling sunlight, she awoke from a disturbing dream in which she was being taken to an emergency room with a needle full of heroin stuck in her arm, while protesting to the emergency medical workers that she had never used heroin in her life. As soon as her eyes were fully open, however, she realized that she was hearing the sound of a real siren in the courtyard. For a moment, she was entirely disoriented, but as she moved, the big picture book fell off her lap, and she remembered everything that had happened before she'd dozed off. Walking into the hall, she saw Harris holding the door open. He was only partially visible until he went to close the door, at which point he looked at her and she saw that there were tears in his eyes.

"Harris! What's going on?" she asked, not really wanting to hear the answer.

"I couldn't wake her," he said.

—*15*—

For the few moments it took for Joanna to say something, the world seemed to stand still for her. When she finally spoke, it was at such a low volume that, if not for the amplification produced by the great hall, she might have been inaudible.

"Wha—what are you saying? She isn't—"

"Oh, no. The situation is serious, but Mrs. Livingston is expected to recover. They're taking her for observation and tests and—hopefully nothing more."

Joanna felt so relieved that she took hold of the library door as if to prevent herself from falling.

"Oh, thank God!" she said. "I don't know what I would've done. I don't think I could bear to lose her now."

"Of course," said Harris—adding, in a rare moment of candor, "I'm not sure what I would have done myself."

"So, um," said Joanna, who was still having to improvise the unfamiliar rules of familiarity, "so then—I guess I should head to the hospital?"

"I couldn't say, Miss Joanna," said Harris, resuming his customary formality. "However, they did say there would be no way to see her until tomorrow. And, of course, Mrs. Livingston never likes one to make a fuss."

"Mrs. Livingston isn't calling the shots right now," said Joanna, as decisively and yet gently as possible.

"No, of course not," said Harris, who was about to excuse himself before remembering to inquire about Joanna's dinner plans.

"Oh, I won't have dinner here," she said, "but thank you for asking."

As he started to walk away, Harris couldn't help adding "Would there be anything else I might—"

"No, Harris. There is nothing you can do for me. Wait—actually that's not true. There *is* something you can do. You can take the evening off and do whatever you need to do for yourself. You can do that for me."

"Oh, I don't think I—" he began, before she interrupted him again.

"That's an order," said Joanna. Then, seeing the look of discomfort that had replaced the look of sadness on his face, she walked over and took his hand. "You really don't know how to take an evening off, do you?" she asked. He didn't answer, but gave her hand a gentle squeeze and walked away.

Once Harris had gone, Joanna walked back into the library, closed the door, and fell against it.

"Please God!" she said. "Please don't let her—please let her be okay! Please don't let her—please don't let anything happen to her. She's all I have. She's been so good to me. Please, please, let her be okay."

At that point, the only thing Joanna was sure of was that she needed a friend. For a moment, she thought of calling Pace, but then she remembered that she'd made plans with Pamela for the evening, and called her instead. Luckily, Pamela had just finished work and was heading to her car. After being brought up to date on the situation, she offered to pick Joanna up and take her to the hospital, where she would be glad to sit with her as long as necessary.

Joanna was not used to having friends who were always available and reliable, and she said a silent prayer of gratitude for Pamela after they hung up. She not only liked Pamela—she also found her fascinating for a number of reasons. First and foremost, they had their addictions in common, which was what had brought them together to begin with. Then there was Pamela's story. Having grown up in a poor African-American family, Pamela had worked her way through college, earning a degree in fashion design and then moving to New York City, where she discovered that she still loved fashion but hated the fashion industry. Through a friend, she had managed to get a job as a makeup artist for a cable news network. While watching to see how the women's makeup looked on camera, Pamela began to listen, more and more intently, to the political positions the women advocated for, and thereby stumbled inadvertently onto what was to become her true passion in life. Before long, she found herself taking an LSAT and going to law school, while continuing to make up the faces of the newswomen and commentators, whom she increasingly peppered with questions. And now she was working for a local chapter of the ACLU, and was involved in every progressive political cause she could make time for, both professionally and privately.

As the two women sat talking in a waiting room at the hospital, they didn't notice that there was quite a bit of interest in them from most of the men who passed by—but after they finished discussing more serious topics, Pamela noticed a couple of cute young doctors, one of whom was white and one of whom was black, who seemed to be lurking in the area, and she nudged Joanna to look at them.

"I think I could go for the salt if you'd go for the pepper," she said, which made Joanna laugh in a way that made the young doctors feel that their interest was being ridiculed, or at least rebuffed by the two women, after which they turned away and returned to their rounds. As a result, Joanna didn't get a good look at either of the young men.

"Oh, no!" said Joanna, "We scared them off."

"Yeah, I tend to do that," said Pamela. "Anyway, I don't have time for pickups in my life right now. Wait a minute—what am I saying? Pickups are the *only* thing I have time for in my life right now!"

"Oh? And how's that working out for you?"

"It's not working out at all," said Pamela. "Which is just fine."

"Well at least you love your work," said Joanna, remembering that Pamela had previously implied that she wasn't much interested in marriage, and definitely not interested in having children.

"Speaking of which, how's the search going for you?" Pamela asked.

"Do you mean men or work?"

"Both, I guess—now that you mention it."

Although it wasn't as easy to evade questions with Pamela as it was with others, Joanna managed, with an "Ugh," to change the subject to their mutual progress in psychotherapy. She had previously told Pamela about her awkward moment with Derek, and was happy to report that it seemed to make no difference at all in their relationship, except that she felt even freer to be completely honest with him.

As the evening progressed and it became clear that no news was likely to be forthcoming, Joanna encouraged Pamela to go ahead and attend the meeting they had planned to attend together, which Pamela reluctantly agreed to do, while diplomatically expressing her concern about the fact that Joanna didn't want to come along.

Pamela had unintentionally redirected Joanna's tendency to obsessive thinking toward the subject of men—or, more specifically, toward the subject of romance—and thus toward Pace Hamilton. Even though she'd been so quick, outwardly, to dismiss him a few hours earlier, after taking a taxi back to Windstone, she called him. When he answered, he was working at the bar, but after hearing a brief rundown of the circumstances (plus Joanna's admission that she was feeling a bit lonely), he said he would call her right back, which he did a couple of minutes later. As it happened, an off-duty coworker of his was hanging out at the bar and had agreed to take his shift for the night, and he told Joanna that he would see her shortly.

When Pace arrived, Harris was just walking through the courtyard on his way out, but returned to the door to let him in. He told Pace that he would find Miss Joanna in the library, and Pace proceeded to knock on the door.

"Come in," said Joanna. She was sitting in Louisa's usual spot on the settee that faced the door. On the table in front of her was a half empty bottle of brandy and a snifter containing a generous portion of the substance.

"Looks like you *really* decided to hold the Coke this time," said Pace, unable to conceal his disappointment. "How much have you had?"

"None," said Joanna. "I poured that symbolically—for my grandmother. At least, that's what I told myself."

"Well, in that case," said Pace, "under the circumstances, maybe you should have just a little."

"Trust me, I wouldn't have just a little—especially under the circumstances. That's not how it works."

"Should I remove the temptation, then?"

"That would be nice, thanks."

After Pace had moved the bottle and glass to the bar area, he started to sit on the settee across from Joanna, but she reached for his hand and guided him to sit next to her.

"Oh, Pace," she said wistfully, "why does stuff like this have to happen? I mean, yes, people get sick and everybody has to die eventually, but with me—people seem to go away just when I need them the most. And, yes, I know this is not about me, but—this afternoon—she told me I'd brought love back into her life. And now, who knows?"

"I hear you," he said, "but if anything bad happens, isn't it great that you were able to give her something that really mattered to her?"

"The thing is, I only got to know her recently. I've ignored her for most of my life."

"But, then, isn't it great that you had what you had?"

"What? A happy ending?"

"Yeah. Maybe. At least you had *something*—if that's how it turns out. I mean, if it turns out that the last interaction you had with her made her happy—"

Joanna appeared to be giving serious consideration to his words before she spoke, and she could see that he was expecting a serious answer.

"Are you hungry?" she asked.

"Um—sure. I wouldn't mind," he said, visibly taken aback.

"I know," she said. "Whiplash, right? Violent change of topic. Welcome to my world. I'm sorry, but all I've had to eat today was that pastry we shared this morning and a couple of tea sandwiches. God, I'm such a hot mess."

"Come on," he said, "give yourself a break. Your grandmother's just been taken to the hospital. You're entitled to be kind of a mess."

"Yeah, but I've been kind of a mess for—kind of forever."

"Alright. So how does pizza sound?" he said, picking up her tactic of steering away from unpleasant topics.

"Pizza sounds like heaven," she said, and as he pulled out his phone to find the number, she added, "That's so great—that you can make snap decisions like that. I vacillate over *everything*."

"Ooh—vacillate—another fancy word," he said. "But I'm sure you're able to make snap decisions."

"Oh, I do," she said, "but they're not pretty."

After the order had been placed, Joanna had the "crazy idea" that they should have their pizza in the immense formal dining room, which Pace said sounded "very civilized." While he paid the delivery boy, Joanna was setting up the paper plates, plastic cups and utensils, along with a two-liter bottle of Diet Coke at the far end of a table that had been designed to seat as many as forty guests and two hosts.

"My ancestors must be turning over in their graves right now," she said, once she'd made things look as formal as possible. "This room was designed for entertaining royalty—with, you know, 12-course French meals."

"Maybe it'll be okay if we say *bon appétit,*" he said.

"Works for me. Shall we dig in?"

"Oh, yeah!"

Joanna had been having her meals at the rehab or with Louisa for so long that she had almost forgotten how much she loved pizza.

"Mmm!" she said. "This pizza is amazing!"

"I know the chef."

"Of course you do. You know, I didn't think I could feel good tonight but—I'm really glad you're here."

"I'm glad you're here, too."

Joanna leaned his way with such a longing sigh that it made him uncomfortable—mainly because he wasn't entirely sure if it was meant for him or whether she was still reacting to the pizza.

"What?" he said.

"I don't know. You're just so uncomplicated."

"Nobody's uncomplicated. I just roll with it."

"So then—aren't you saying that life is complicated, but that you're not?"

"Nope. No sale."

"Damn! Another fairytale bites the dust. Anyway, it must be nice—rolling with the punches. Doesn't work for me."

"Have you tried?"

"I like to think so. Maybe there've just been too many punches."

"Maybe you need to step out of the ring once in a while."

Joanna wasn't sure if Pace was being glib or whether he was taking her seriously. Either way, it made her uncomfortable, and she spoke before thinking it through.

"I think we're on the verge of what you writers call torturing the metaphor."

"Hmm. No wonder you get punched," he said, a little too casually.

Now she was beyond mere discomfort. She wondered if that awful moment had arrived when what seems too good to be true turns out to be just that.

"Excuse me?" she said indignantly.

"Calm down," he said, stroking her hand, "I didn't mean punched literally. I meant punched by life—not that that's a whole lot better—because I assumed that's what *you* meant. I'm sorry. I really didn't mean any harm."

This time, she took a moment to weigh her reaction.

"No, I'm the one who should be sorry," she said.

"Just this once," he said, "let *me* be sorry."

"Ok, just this once," she said, smiling at him until he smiled back. "Boy—you sure can't call *me* uncomplicated."

"There's no way I can respond to that without getting in trouble."

"I wasn't expecting a response," she said, "but that was kind of perfect."

"Really? How so? You know—for future reference."

"Because it was simple and spontaneous. I wish I could do that more often. I just have so much baggage."

"Like what? I mean, apart from the split personality."

"Like—um," she said, trying to adopt a lighter tone, "like I don't think I've ever had sex without being high on something. The idea of even trying it scares the hell out of me."

"Hmm," he said.

"Hmm?" she said. "I think I'm gonna need some footnotes here."

Pace took a moment to cautiously gather his thoughts.

"Well, let's see. I guess my take on that is that—for you—having sex without drugs and alcohol would be like—well, kind of like having sex for the first time, right?"

"Oh, God. What must that make me sound like to you?"

"Vulnerable," he said without hesitation.

"Okay," she said, "I just died."

With that, she moved her chair closer to his, took his hand, and began kissing him. To her surprise, as well as his own, it was Pace who put the brakes on things. He reached for his beverage, took a long swill, and sat back.

"I can stay over, if you need me to," he said. "I'll stay until you want me to leave."

"I can't imagine wanting you to leave, but—"

"It's okay. You don't have to explain. I meant I would stay over as a friend—just so you'd know somebody was nearby. You're too fragile for anything else right now. I'm guessing there's an extra bed or two upstairs?"

"You really are too good to be true. I just know you're going to turn out to be a serial killer."

"Hey—what if that's true?" he said, grinning at her. "Like, what if I *am* a serial killer but I don't even know it yet myself—like—maybe you're my first victim?"

"Whatever," she said. "Finish your pizza."

—16—

After what they jokingly referred to as doing the dishes, Joanna took Pace to the landing at the top of the stairs to choose a bedroom. It was barely 10:00 p.m. but, despite her long nap, Joanna had already begun yawning. Pace professed to being a little sleepy as well, which wasn't true, but he knew Joanna was probably exhausted from her day, and also that there was a library downstairs to keep him busy.

"Let's see," she said, glancing about, "I know there are a few empty bedrooms near mine. This is my room, by the way. It's called the Blue Room—although there's nothing blue in it—and strangely, my grandmother doesn't seem to know why."

Then the obvious choice came to mind.

"This one should be ok," she said.

"Looks fine to me."

"This was my grandfather's room."

"Really?"

"Yeah. No one's slept here for a long time, but I know it was just cleaned. Not sure if there are any sheets, though."

"Don't worry about it," he said. "I'll be fine."

"I'm sorry," she said. "I feel like I'm deserting you."

"I'm fine. Really."

"Okay, well—thanks again."

"Do you want to lock me out from the inside—just in case?"

"Stop it," she said. "You'll give me nightmares."

She gave him a quick kiss and then scurried with mock fear into her room, after which she made a lot of noise with the lock.

"Just kidding," she shouted from the other side. "I locked it, but then I unlocked it."

"Goodnight," he said. "Get some rest."

"You too!" she said.

Pace entered Seth Livingston's bedroom warily, as if he expected to find the old man still there—which in a way he did. There was a strong presence of a particular kind of classical masculine taste that pervaded the decor. On inspecting what seemed to be a freshly made bed, he discovered that there were, in fact, no sheets. But there was a wall full of leather-bound books, mostly classics, with bindings that had hardly been cracked, if at all. Looking up, barely within his reach, he noticed a large book that was slightly askew, and went to straighten it—which caused it to fall to the floor, along with a large manila envelope from which a stack of papers slid out. As he was about to stuff the contents back into the envelope, he noticed a note clipped to the first page, which read:

THE BEST OF LIVES – A NOVEL BY L.W. LIVINGSTON

He seemed to recall hearing Harris refer to Joanna's grandmother as Mrs. Livingston earlier, and wondered if this could be a manuscript of the novel Joanna had told him about.

As a general rule, Pace was anything but nosey—but he wasn't without curiosity, particularly when it came to the subject of literature. While he was debating with himself whether or not to delve further, he was respectfully but reluctantly rearranging the contents back into the envelope.

But there was something odd about this. He wasn't normally the sort of person to feel premonitions, yet he felt a premonition about this. He pulled the contents back out of the envelope.

The note was attached to a cover letter which, somewhat guiltily, he couldn't resist reading. It read:

WINDSTONE

August 27, 1950

Dear Harry,

Enclosed you will find a copy of Louisa's manuscript, which I hope you will find to have merit. She's so excited by the prospect of your reading it that she's hovering over my shoulder even as I write this. Thank you again for making the time. We will, of course, eagerly await your response.

With all good wishes,

Seth Livingston

Pace took another look at the manila envelope. It was addressed to J. Harriman Arden at Stuyvesant Publishing in New York City. Then he looked at the upper right-hand corner of the envelope.

"Hmm," he said out loud. "No postage."

In a flash, he conjectured what must have been the fate of the manuscript. Slipping off his shoes and socks and putting the envelope and notes aside, he made himself comfortable on top of the bed and began to read Louisa's novel.

It began with a prologue that, while well-written, was so allegorical as to be inscrutable. It was also mercifully brief. When the narrative got underway, however, almost from the start, he found himself completely absorbed in it. Even before the storyline began to engage him, he was captivated by the writing style—which had the rare attribute of being conversational and yet quite formal—in a way that reminded him of Edith Wharton. The characters were diverse and intriguing, and they spoke in what seemed like authentic individual voices—an aspect of writing that had always eluded Pace in his attempts at fiction. Within a few hours, he had finished the entire novel, which was really more of a novella, after which he sat for a while in a satisfying meditative trance, until he thought he heard moaning coming from the room next door. Tossing the manuscript aside, he left the room to go check on Joanna. As he entered the hall, the moaning accelerated into a near scream. Rushing into Joanna's room, he arrived at the side of her bed and took hold of her just as she was about to wake up.

"Hey, Joanna, wake up!" he said. "Are you okay?"

"Oh, my god, Pace!" she said. "I was having the worst nightmare. It was horrible."

"I can see that," he said. "But you're okay now."

"But it was so horrible."

"It must have been to make you scream like that. Do you want to tell me about it?"

"It was just—I don't even remember most of it but—at one point—my grandfather was strangling my grandmother. I guess it's because she's in the hospital and you were in his room, but it was really disturbing."

"Yeah, that would be disturbing."

He was longing to tell her about the manuscript, especially given the eerie coincidence of her dream, but he'd been on the verge of being half asleep himself, so instead, he just patted her on the back and comforted her.

"Hey, you know what?" he said. "This is a really big bed and—I'm still dressed and you're kinda half-dressed. So how about if I just sleep on top of the covers on the other side there? Would that make you feel safer?"

"That would be great, but—"

"I promise nothing's gonna to happen. Except sleep. Hopefully."

"Okay sure, that sounds good. But we probably shouldn't cuddle, right?

"Right. No cuddling. Now try to sleep."

"Okay, good night."

"Goodnight," he said—and soon they were both sound asleep.

—17—

Joanna had gone to bed without closing the heavy brocade curtains which, along with the draping around her bed, had been designed to keep the room as dark as a tomb—all day long if necessary. In the days when great balls were given, the festivities often started after a lengthy dinner and continued through the night, followed by breakfast and finally a sleep that could stretch well into the daytime. So, when the unobstructed early morning light began to permeate the room, she gradually began to open her eyes.

After the mild shock of the intruding sunlight, the next thing she became aware of was that Pace, although still on top of the covers, was spooning her. For a split-second, she found it alarming. It brought back a horrible feeling from the past, when she wasn't always sure of the identity of the person who was lying next to her in bed. But then she remembered who it was and why he was there—which brought a smile to her face as she pulled the arm that was wrapped around her even tighter. At that, Pace opened his eyes.

"Good morning," he whispered into her ear.

"Good morning."

"Did the second half of the night go any better for you? I didn't hear any screams."

"Much better. Thanks to you."

"Well that's good."

"And did you sleep well?"

"Pretty well. I had some strange dreams, but no nightmares."

"It's funny—I almost never have nightmares," she said. "At least, not when I'm sleeping."

"Oh, no. It's too early for that wit of yours," he said.

"Well, too bad. It goes with the package—along with what you call my split personality."

"Fair enough," he said, "But it would be easier if we could rustle up some coffee."

"I think I can manage that," she said, before rolling over to plant a quick kiss on him, after which she sprang out of bed and headed downstairs, with Pace following along.

When they were about halfway down the stairs, the front door opened, and in walked Louisa, who paused in the doorway to savor the great hall as if she were making a triumphal return after a long absence. Almost immediately, though, her attention was diverted to the staircase.

Joanna was wearing a tank top tee-shirt and a pair of large men's flannel boxers that had belonged to Danny, while Pace was wearing very wrinkled chinos with an unbuttoned shirt. They were both barefoot. As Joanna rushed downstairs to embrace her and ask how she was feeling, Louisa appeared to view the unexpected scene with good grace, and yet with the theatricality of a grande dame whose big entrance has just been upstaged.

"I'm fine, thanks," she said. "considering I didn't get a wink of sleep—what with monitoring this and testing that! What a lot of fuss." Then, whispering in Joanna's ear, she added, "I hope I'm not interrupting anything."

"Don't say a word," Joanna whispered to her, "I'll tell you all about it later."

"You're damn right you will," Louisa whispered back, "Omitting no detail."

"Granny, stop that! And please don't say well, well, well."

"Well—well—*well*," said Louisa out loud. Then, turning back to Joanna, she whispered "I said it to him. Not to you."

"Good morning, Mrs. Livingston," said Pace, blushing. "I'm sorry. This is kind of embarrassing."

"Oh, really?" she said. "I think it's very interesting!"

"Granny, seriously," said Joanna.

Louisa had left the front door open and, at that moment, a car door slammed in the courtyard.

"Who's that?" Joanna asked, worried that Louisa might have been compelled to bring home a healthcare worker.

"It's Harris," said Louisa. "He was paying the taxi."

"Oh, of course he would come to pick you up," said Joanna.

"He didn't come to pick me up," said Louisa. "He spent the night at the hospital."

As Harris walked into the hall and closed the door behind him, Joanna gave him an eloquent look, after which she walked over and kissed him.

"Oh, my," said Louisa, in a loud whisper directed at Pace. "Isn't she fickle?"

"Good morning, everyone," said Harris, as perplexed by the gathering as he was by the dress code. "Would anyone care for breakfast?"

"You want to make us breakfast after you've been up all night?" said Joanna in astonishment.

"Well, Miss Joanna—to be honest—I'm rather hungry myself. So, if you'll excuse me," he said, starting toward the back of the house.

"Don't you even think of cooking anything for us," Louisa yelled after him. "You just throw some cold things onto the buffet table and we'll serve ourselves! Then, turning to Pace, lest he should be shocked, she added, "We have a cook, of course, but she only comes in for dinner. Alright then, everyone. To the breakfast room."

As they reached the back of the hall, the doorbell rang. Harris was about to return to answer the door, but Joanna stopped him.

"No, you go on," she said, "I'll get it."

When she opened the door, Pamela was standing there, looking far from her best.

"Pamela!" said Joanna, forgetting the resonance of the hall, which caused Pace to turn around.

"I'm so sorry," said Pamela. "I've been trying to call you. I really need a friend right now."

"Is everything okay?" said Pace—which caused Pamela to take a deep breath.

"Yeah, sure," said Joanna. "Go on in. I'll join you in a few minutes."

"Who was that?" Pamela asked. She was now completely unnerved.

"Just a friend," said Joanna.

"Yeah—well your friend tried to rape me last night."

PART THREE

—18—

After a less than pleasant freshman year, Pace Hamilton was looking forward to his sophomore year. His freshman year had been fraught with indecision and anxiety. The indecision was mostly about his choice of a major. He had postponed making that decision because of a dispute with his father, who simply couldn't understand why his son would choose such an excellent school and yet waste his time studying literature—especially in a department that was known for promoting innovative and avant-garde literature. Mr. Hamilton was all for innovation—as long as it conduced to the accumulation of great wealth—but the very word avant-garde, regardless of the context, was anathema to him.

Mrs. Hamilton, on the other hand, was tacitly in support of her son's decision; but when it came to decisions of any magnitude or lasting consequence, she invariably deferred to her husband. Owing to a pre-nuptial agreement which, in the event of a divorce, would make it impossible for her to enjoy anything remotely like her present lifestyle, she had long since decided not to rock the boat—at least not to the point where it could begin taking on water. The Barclay-Hamilton marriage was not an unhappy one, but it had always felt more like a business arrangement; one in which both parties understood and accepted the advantages of playing their respective roles. For her part, Caroline Hamilton was a celebrated hostess and, even in middle age, a world-famous beauty. And her husband, for his part, was filthy rich.

But the anxiety that had pervaded Pace's freshman year was mostly due to having had his identical twin brother Barclay as a roommate. Barclay, who insisted on being called Clay because he hated having his mother's maiden name as his first name, had been in a pre-med program the previous year, but there had been some unpleasant events which had made his removal from Providence advisable.

Unlike his brother, Clay Hamilton was more interested in being known as the life of a party than as an excellent student. It was at an off-campus party that he had met a "smoking hot" young waitress who enjoyed partying as much as himself. One night, toward the end of his first semester, when he was very drunk and she was nearly unconscious, he had date-raped the girl without the usual protection, and had got her pregnant. Despite her penchant for the wild side, the girl was a devout Catholic who refused even to consider the option of an abortion, which led to a series of unpleasant meetings and sordid negotiations. Mr. Hamilton, for whom Clay could do no wrong, was convinced that the girl had entrapped his favorite son. Nevertheless, an exorbitant financial settlement had been reached, and Clay had been transferred to a university in Manhattan, where he was compelled to live at home under the watchful eyes of his parents.

And now Pace had a new roommate, a classmate of his named Jason Levinson, who was also his best friend, or, as Jason liked to say, "his spiritual twin—not to be confused with his evil twin." Above all, Jason shared Pace's passion for literature—although his tastes inclined to the traditional western canon, whereas Pace was generally more attracted to novelties—what Jason called novel novels. In fact, the two boys were much more inclined to talk about literature than the conventional college boy topics of sex, booze, sports and music. This made both of them occasionally wonder if something was wrong with them, which was the only area of mutual concern that they never discussed openly. Neither of them showed any interest in the party scene, and both of them were universally regarded as outstanding students with considerable potential. Interestingly, Pace always said that

Jason possessed the greater talent as a writer, whereas Jason said the same thing about Pace (while inwardly agreeing with Pace's assessment).

Pace and Jason had been best friends since attending prep school together at the Collegiate School in Manhattan. Indeed, it was Jason who had first encouraged Pace's nascent literary aspirations, and who had stood by him as he stood up to his father. The Levinsons were not, like the Hamiltons, merely major benefactors to the arts and humanities, but passionate subscribers as well—and they were thrilled by the idea of the two boys pursuing writing careers. No one had the poor taste to say it out loud, but it was understood that both Jason and Pace would have the financial backing that would allow them to take as much time as they needed to pursue and develop their art. Mrs. Levinson—who thought of the boys almost as a couple—had once, at a dinner party she was giving for a famous historian, referred to the boys as Damon and Pythias.

"Wrong school," said Jason to his mother, "Damon and Pythias were Syracusan. We're going to Brown."

"This," said one admiring guest to another, "is what constitutes dinner conversation in the Levinson household."

Therefore, from the Levinsons' point of view, now that the two boys had achieved their longtime goal of living together while pursuing their shared passion for learning, everything was for the best in the best of all possible worlds.

Jason had found them a small apartment on Thayer Street that made for a short walk to classes, and an even shorter walk to all their favorite fast-food restaurants—which was expedient, as neither of them could boil an egg. From the start, the atmosphere was almost idyllic. Long and overly earnest discussions and amicable debates were the order of the day—or more likely the order of the evening—and besides reveling in Jason's company, Pace was happy not to have to babysit his twin brother any longer. For his part, Jason was happy just to be with Pace, whom he had come to regard as his anchor in the world.

Anyone is capable of denial, as long as it satisfies a desire, or even perhaps a genuine need, without encroaching too forcefully on one's intuition—and, despite his capacity for keen observation, Pace Hamilton was no exception. Even after a thousand indications and innuendos, he had never admitted to himself that his best friend was gay and—more to the point—that his best friend was desperately in love with him. The fact that Jason himself was still somewhat in denial may have contributed to Pace's denial, but Jason's denial was now beginning to wear thin.

The two of them could easily have afforded a two-bedroom apartment, and yet when Jason extolled the coziness that would be afforded them by a shared bedroom, Pace was all in for the idea. After all, there were two beds. But for Jason, it wasn't just the quasi-cohabiting aspect of sharing a bedroom that mattered—although that was paramount—it was also the thought, only dimly acknowledged, that if Pace had his own room, he might one day bring a girl to his room. And that eventuality was too excruciating to be consciously considered.

He'd seen Pace undressed countless times. After all, they'd worked out together and gone skiing, sailing and swimming together. But they'd never slept in the same room. In all those previous circumstances, Jason had somehow managed to convince himself that his occasional "impure thoughts" signified nothing more than a phase he was going through, after which he was always able read himself peacefully to sleep.

But this was different. In the past, Pace had always shown a tendency to be tactile in his affections toward everyone he loved, including Jason. Now, he seemed more circumspect about the ways in which they touched. In purely physical terms, if he had had any inclination to experiment with homosexuality, Jason would have been the ideal partner for Pace. The problem was that he truly loved Jason, and it was that deep but platonic love which, ironically, rendered Jason the last person on earth he would have experimented with, even if he were so-inclined—which, in any case, he was not.

One night, after the two of them had been studying a work of Oscar Wilde's, they discussed the subject of homosexuality for the first and only time. After a few beers, Pace confessed—with no awareness of the unintended harm he was causing—that Jason was the only male with whom he could ever imagine being physically intimate; although he hastened to assure him (to reassure him, he thought) that such a thing could never, ever happen.

That night, Jason didn't sleep. Until then, he hadn't fully acknowledged to himself that he was gay. He had managed to convince himself that his occasional interest in other boys was no more than a side-effect of his abiding—yet hopefully transient—fondness for Pace. But now he could see that it was the other way around. The object of his love, and now of his lust as well, was sleeping an arm's reach away from him in the next bed. In the darkest part of the night, he almost persuaded himself to make a move. He was fairly sure that, being a bit drunk as well as being a total mensch, Pace would acquiesce and throw himself into the spirit of it. That would be wonderful, of course—for the moment. But what would the morning bring? Guilt and recriminations. Or, more likely, Pace would just be his sweet self and write the whole thing off to life experience while Jason laughingly blamed it all on Oscar Wilde. Somehow, he felt, that would be even harder to bear. The only thing he was sure of was that, going forward, the status quo would be unacceptable. But what was he to do? He had no idea.

As it turned out, that decision was not left to him. It wasn't long after that that Pace found himself a girlfriend.

The girl, whose name was Carly, was a sweet, red-haired beauty from Charleston, South Carolina. As was the case with Pace, it was virtually impossible not to like her, and she had been one of the few classmates with whom Jason himself was particularly close, and he now hated the fact that he'd always spoken so highly of her to Pace—and hated himself even more for descending to such a bitter, jealous thought. More and more, after they all returned from the winter holiday break, Pace began spending evenings, and then nights, with Carly.

For Jason, every element of the situation became another form of torture. Even hearing people refer to "Pace and Carly," was unbearable—in part because it sounded so mellifluous. Strangely, the least terrible part was when Pace spoke to Jason of his feelings for Carly. If nothing else, that usually meant that he and Pace were alone together. But the worst of it came when Carly began making efforts to become closer to Jason. They'd already been good friends, and—after all—who better to talk to endlessly about Pace than his best friend? But hearing Carly talk about a relationship he could never have was agonizing. Soon, however, as Pace began spending every night with Carly, that particular aspect of the torture came to an end.

The odd nights he'd spent alone had been barely tolerable for Jason, but being alone now every night only compounded his feeling of loneliness. Yet he craved isolation. For the first time ever, he had difficulty studying, or even maintaining his interest in studying. Then he began, here and there, skipping a few of his favorite classes. Then he began skipping classes altogether, which caused Pace to look in on him to see if he was alright. Initially, the kindness and love Pace showed toward him in those visits was like the breath of life to Jason, but soon they became inexplicably onerous. Now, alone every day and every night, he was more and more bereft of inspiration and motivation. Sometimes, he would fantasize that Pace was just working something out in himself, after which he would return to him a new man, and profess his love for Jason above all others. Such fantasies, alas, were always followed by the same hard dose of reality that returned him to the depths of despair. He had always suffered from depression, sometimes severe depression, but he had always had the most attentive, caring parents—and the best friend anyone could imagine.

Just before the Easter break, following up on a call from Mrs. Levinson, Pace stopped by the apartment in the hope of finding Jason. After the first responders had taken Jason's body from the apartment, Pace sat down, still in shock, and wondered how he could possibly convey the news to Jason's parents. On the table next to him was Jason's favorite book, *The Age of Innocence*. He picked it up and mindlessly flipped through its pages, which were dog-eared and highlighted everywhere. Then he cried—as he had never cried before.

—19—

For a moment, Joanna just stared at Pamela. She was still barely awake, and would have preferred this to be another bad dream. The past twenty-four hours had been something of an emotional roller coaster and, now that Louisa was safely back at home, Joanna was ready for a day without drama. But as Pamela's accusation about Pace quickly sank in, her newfound optimism was beginning to plummet. Then—if not for Pamela, at least for Pace—a silver lining occurred to her.

"Wait," she said, "that's not possible. He was here all evening. And all night." Then, she thought for a moment and added. "I mean—"

"You mean—what?" said Pamela, as if she were cross-examining a witness.

"I mean—I went to bed kind of early, and he didn't join me until much later—sometime in the middle of the night. But we had dinner together, and I'm sure—"

"What time did you go to bed?"

"I don't know. Maybe ten? Maybe ten-thirty?"

"And where was he then?"

"Well," Joanna began, with what appeared to be deliberate obfuscation, but was actually her hesitancy to reveal the details of the preceding night, which now sounded almost juvenile, and which she was sure would strike Pamela as unconvincing. "He was—I mean, I guess—"

"What the fuck is going on here, Jo?" said Pamela. She was normally an exceptionally pleasant person, but she was understandably still shaken, and becoming annoyed as well. Joanna reluctantly explained as much of the timeline from the previous night as she was certain of, and explained why she couldn't account for her "friend" for what turned out to be a critical portion of the evening. Pamela then recounted how she'd left her car in the hospital parking lot and walked to the meeting, after which she joined some of the other attendees for a late meal. At around eleven o'clock, she had returned to the hospital to pick up her car, which was when Joanna's "friend" accosted her.

"You think you're so hot, don't you?" he had said to her, as he grabbed her and spun her around. At the time, she was still dressed for work—in a pants suit—and thus the comment wasn't likely to be a reference to the way she was dressed. Then he asked "Where's your girlfriend?" which meant nothing to Pamela except a possible case of mistaken identity or, more likely, that this guy was on some kind of drugs. He had grabbed her with a violent force, and he now began feeling her up in the most invasive way. He was a tall, powerfully built young man and, just as Pamela was wishing she hadn't dropped out of a course in self-defense after only one class, she remembered the pepper spray in her purse, and deployed it to full effect. As the young man howled and cursed at her and stumbled away, she let herself into her car, locked the door, reached for her phone, which she'd left in the car, and called the police.

After Pamela concluded her account, Joanna—who was now shaken herself—excused herself, saying she'd better go talk to Pace. Pamela said that that probably wasn't the best idea, preferring instead to set the wheels of law enforcement into immediate motion.

"Please," said Joanna, "Just give me a couple of minutes."

Against her better judgement, Pamela agreed, reaching in her bag for her phone in order to keep it at the ready. As Joanna walked away, Pamela remembered, in the strange way people remember otherwise seemingly insignificant details in the aftermath of a crime, about the two cute young doctors from the evening before, and was sure that the man who assaulted her was one of them. No wonder Joanna seemed so dodgy about the details of her evening. She'd apparently brought one of the doctors home with her.

But then, why did he return to the hospital parking lot? And at that hour?

As she approached the breakfast room, Joanna could hear laughter, which was soon eclipsed by the sound of Louisa's voice, who seemed to be regaling the company with an anecdote about something. When she saw Joanna's face, she stopped laughing.

"Oh, my dear!" she said. "Such a long face. Are you alright?"

"I'm sorry," said Joanna to everyone. Then she addressed Pace directly. "Um—can I talk with you for a minute? It's really important."

"So possessive!" Louisa joked to Harris, who was pouring coffee. "She won't let him out of her sight for a minute."

Joanna attempted a tense smile, but could find no humor in the situation.

"I'll be back shortly," she said, walking over to kiss her grandmother on the check. "Welcome home, Granny."

By now, even Louisa could see that something was more than routinely amiss—and she didn't fail to notice that Joanna had *not* said "*We* will back shortly."

As Joanna took Pace into the hallway that led back toward the great hall, he stopped for a moment and asked her if everything was alright, knowing of course that it wasn't. Her plan had been to have a few words with him first, but she couldn't yet clear her head enough to figure out exactly what she should say. Instead, she told him that her friend needed to ask him about an urgent matter. Unfortunately for Pace, urgent matters involving mistaken identity between him and his brother had a way of cropping up with depressing regularity, and something instinctual now told him that this could be one of them.

As they approached the front door, Pamela stood up stiffly and clutched her phone tightly, while Joanna made a terse formal introduction. Pamela went straight to the heart of the matter, informing Pace that she was about to file charges against him, and that she could positively identify him as a sexual predator who had assaulted her the previous night in the hospital parking lot. She was about to dial her phone when Pace begged her to listen to him for a minute. When he heard the mention of the hospital, any lingering doubt he may have had about the situation was removed. He quickly explained, to Joanna's astonishment and Pamela's incredulity, that he had an identical twin brother who was an intern at that hospital. Pamela had to stifle the impulse to laugh at what seemed to her such a farcical alibi.

"Oh, *really*," she said with disgust, "and he just happened to attack *me* while you were here with *my* friend?"

Like Joanna, he was still barely awake, and all he could think of to say at that moment was "It's a small town," which annoyed Joanna enough to join the conversation.

"So, wait a minute," she said, "You're telling us that you have—like—an evil twin?"

For an instant, Pace's late friend Jason flashed through his mind. Jason had used those very words, albeit jokingly, back in college.

"Well," said Pace, "actually—yes, I am."

Pamela was about to take charge of the proceedings again, but just as she was about to speak, the wheels of her legal mind began to spin. She had unleashed a considerable dose of pepper spray into the eyes or her assailant, and she knew that the effects could range from mere burning to temporary blindness, and that they lasted anywhere from thirty minutes to two hours. As unlikely as Pace's alibi may have seemed to her, it now seemed equally unlikely that he would have been able to drive back to Joanna's house, and slide into bed with her without having some residual effects in his eyes. As much as she didn't want to—she was forced to at least consider his story.

"What's your brother's name?" she asked.

"Clay Hamilton," he said, "Uh, Barclay Hamilton, actually."

The hospital's number was programmed into Pamela's phone. As she began dialing, she said, "There'd better be an intern at that hospital named Barclay Hamilton."

Once the existence of Pace's twin had been established to her satisfaction, Pamela wanted to be anywhere else but in the great hall of Windstone. She apologized to both Pace and Joanna—both of whom said no apology was necessary. Joanna asked her, awkwardly but sincerely, if she wanted to stay for breakfast—but, in addition to still being shaken by the events of the preceding night, Pamela was so embarrassed that she felt compelled to leave immediately—with a quick hug to Joanna and a quick shake of Pace's hand. "Sorry again," she said, as she darted out the door. Joanna asked her if she needed her to come along, but Pamela waved her hand without looking back.

For an instant, the two of them stood there, wondering who should speak first and what they should say. Pace now had a worried look on his face. Accustomed as he had become to his brother's behavior, he knew that this would be different. This was no waitress who could be placated by receiving adequate child-support, and he could readily imagine that all hell was about to break loose at Hamilton Court. As much as she needed a hug herself, it was apparent to Joanna that he needed one more. She hugged him tightly and said, "I'm so sorry for that."

"Don't be sorry," he said. "I'm just sorry for your friend."

"I really want to go after her—in case she needs moral support. But she's one of those people who wants to be left alone when things go wrong. That's one thing we do *not* have in common."

"I promise I won't feel abandoned if you want to run after her and double-check," he said.

"Let's go have some breakfast," she said—hugging him even more tightly for a moment. "Believe me, when Pamela decides she needs me, she won't hesitate to call."

—20—

The past twenty-four hours had been filled with surprises, and the latest surprise—when Joanna and Pace reentered the breakfast room—was the welcome surprise of seeing Harris seated at the breakfast table across from Louisa. Of course, she had insisted that he join her, and yet she couldn't resist making a joke about it.

"My dears—look!" she said, as they entered the room, "The revolution has come at last! Harris has joined us at the table." Then, seeing the hangdog look on Harris's face, she added, "Poor man—I shouldn't tease you." Then, back to the others, she added, "He looked so tired. I was afraid he'd fall over if he didn't sit down."

Pace and Joanna did their best to put on friendly, carefree faces, but Louisa hadn't been born yesterday.

"Now—what is going on with the two of you?" she asked.

"Oh, we're fine," said Joanna. "I'll tell you all about it later."

"Indeed you will," said Louisa. "In the meantime, I have some exciting news!"

Pace and Joanna poured themselves a much-needed cup of coffee and joined the others at the table. Joanna was almost as desperate for a positive distraction at that moment as she was for the coffee.

"Tell us," she said.

"*Well—*" said Louisa, "I imagine Pace has already told you *his* good news?"

"About the magazine?" said Joanna.

"What magazine?" asked Louisa, looking intrigued.

"Oh, um, no," Pace said to Joanna, "this was something else. I forgot to mention it last night."

"I'm sure you had more pressing things to talk about last night," said Louisa, in a highly suggestive tone.

"Like you being in the hospital?" said Joanna, almost reproachfully.

Louisa patted Joanna's hand in a consoling way, and in a barely audible whisper, mouthed the words "Yes, dear, I'm sorry."

"I'll tell you about it later," Pace said to Joanna.

"*I'll* tell you about it *now*," said Louisa, "if Pace doesn't mind.

"Oh, no—of course not," he said.

"*Well*," said Louisa, "While you were out there doing whatever you were doing with your friend, Pace asked me to appear in a documentary film!"

"A documentary film?" said Joanna. She hadn't been out of bed for more than about fifteen minutes, and already the events of the day were beginning to seem overwhelming.

"Yes!" said Louisa. "It seems that Caroline is making a documentary film about the social history of Newport, and she's asked Pace to write the—what did you call it—the voice above?"

"The voice over," said Pace.

"Oh, that's it, the voice over. *Anyway*, he also wants me to help with the writing—*and*—he wants to interview me. On camera! Isn't it thrilling?"

"Um, yeah," said Joanna dully. "That sounds great."

"Try not to overexcite yourself, my dear," said Louisa.

"I'm sorry," said Joanna, "my mind was somewhere else. Yes, it really sounds exciting, Granny."

"*Well*—you'll probably like it even better when you hear the rest of it." Here, Louisa looked at Pace and nodded toward Joanna, indicating that she was throwing the ball to him.

"Oh, um, yeah," he said, rousing himself slightly, "I told her I was going to ask you to handle the music end of it."

"Oh, sure," said Joanna, still in a tone that was mostly sleepy, but sounded rather glum. "Sounds great."

"For heaven's sake!" said Louisa, "If this is the way you people act when you're planning a film, I'd hate to see you planning a funeral."

"I'm sorry, Granny. It really does sound great. I think we've just all had a rough night."

"Oh, have we?" said Louisa, before realizing she was on the verge of going too far. "I mean, of course we have! But we haven't talked about the other exciting news,"

Harris looked even more uncomfortable than usual as Louisa said this.

"It seems that our beloved Harris has joined an amateur theatrical company."

"Oh, how wonderful!" said Joanna.

"Yes, everyone here seems to have a secret life except for me," said Louisa. "But get this—they're doing *The Importance of Being Earnest* for their next production, and he thinks I might be able to play Lady Bracknell!"

Louisa was the sort of woman who would automatically assume that anyone who was dining with her would be familiar with the most famous character in Oscar Wilde's most famous play. Joanna was fairly sure she'd heard of it somewhere, but acted just as excited as if it were her favorite play. Pace, on the other hand, had actually read the play, during the time when he and Jason were studying Oscar Wilde. But, without the necessary ingredient of seasoned English actors, it hadn't exactly bowled him over. Still, he remembered smiling quite a lot.

Meanwhile, Harris was looking abjectly uncomfortable—not only, as the others might have thought, because he was unused to dining with his employer or that he wasn't comfortable being the center of attention. He was also uncomfortable because he had, in fact, dined with Louisa on a few special occasions in the recent past—*and* he had been doing performances with the community theatre group, off and on, for about twenty years. It was the first occasion he'd ever had to worry about Louisa's memory—but he consoled himself with the thought that she'd just had a serious enough bump on the head to lose consciousness—and neither he nor Louisa told anyone that she had left the hospital against doctors' orders.

"Are you playing Algernon or Jack?" asked Pace, surprising himself with his memory while impressing Joanna mightily and almost startling Harris.

Louisa, who thought Pace was being gallant when, in fact, he was being quite sincere, said “Forsooth, my good man.” (which made Harris finally crack a smile) “He will be playing the Reverend Doctor Chasuble.”

“Oh, of course,” said Pace, only then remembering the somewhat minor character of the older man.

“Alright, then,” said Louisa peremptorily, “I will leave you all to your youthful gloom and lethargy. Some of us have things to do.”

As she got up from the table, Harris and Pace rose with her.

“Sit down!” she snapped. “I didn’t mean you, dear—I meant you, Harris. I *insist* you take the day off and relax. If I see you so much as pick up a spoon for the rest of the day—except that one, of course—you’re fired.”

As she was leaving the room, she stopped behind Harris’s chair and put her hands on his shoulders.

“You’re a good friend, Harris,” she said. “A good and a trusted friend.”

Before she could become emotional, Louisa swept out of the room, leaving Harris also on the verge of tears. When she was gone, he said, “Excuse me, please,” and left Joanna and Pace to themselves.

Once again, neither of them knew exactly what to say about anything, or even which thread to pick up first. They both felt as if they somehow knew each other well, but were equally aware that they were almost total strangers.

“I was serious about you doing the music for the film,” he said at length. He knew that there was more serious business to discuss, especially with regard to her friend and his family, but he felt that a light touch was indicated.

“Yes, I assumed you were,” she said absently. Then, returning to the moment, “How are you?”

“Oh, I’m fine,” he said, which sounded similar to her “Oh, nothing” from the day before. “How are *you*?”

“I’m fine,” she said, a little more persuasively. “A little worried though—about Pamela, and Granny—and you.”

"Don't worry about me," he said, "and your grandmother seems fine. I feel horrible about your friend, though."

"Yeah," she said, "That must be—I don't even know what to say. Do you want to talk about it?"

"I don't know what to say either—but I can listen."

"No, that's okay. I think maybe I should go check on Granny—to see if she needs any help."

"Do you mind if I wait for you here?" he asked.

"Of course not," she said. "Anyway, I'm sure she's fine. She's probably upstairs deciding what to wear to the Oscars already." While he was laughing, she added, "I should at least go put some more clothes on, though—don't you think?"

"You're asking the wrong person about that," he said, raising an eyebrow seductively, which made her laugh. It was nervous laughter on both their parts, mainly because they both realized that they barely knew each other, and weren't sure how to discuss all the external issues that were suddenly, so to speak, on the table.

"So," she said, trying to sound carefree, "what happens now?"

"I don't know," he said, "but I do know I want to spend as much time with you as possible. You've, um, you've kinda made me believe in love at first sight."

"Oh, no!" she said, "Do you know what you're saying?"

"I do," he said.

She'd been trying to hide the fact that she had an inkling of the same feeling herself—and yet, there it was—one more thing on the table.

"Okay, then," she said. "I guess we'll see what happens. But it won't be easy."

"Nothing worthwhile is easy," he said.

"Okay, do you write down things like that in advance, or do you just always say the perfect thing?"

"Haha," he said, "Neither. But—speaking of writing—there's something I ought to tell you."

"Aha," she said, "I knew it was all too good to be true."

"No, it's nothing about the film or the magazine. Oh, hell, I'm just gonna blurt it right out." He took a deep breath and said it.

"I found your grandmother's manuscript."

"You mean—for her book?"

"Yep."

"Where? I mean how?"

"I was looking for something to read last night in your grandfather's room, and I went to move this huge book back into place, and the manuscript fell from behind it onto the floor.

"Wow!" she said. "I mean—*wow!*"

"Yeah, I know."

"I just assumed she would have thrown it away. I guess maybe—my grandfather kept it for sentimental reasons."

"Um, I don't think so."

"Why do you say that?"

"Well, there's more. There was a letter attached to it. A cover letter."

"I don't think I like where this is going," Joanna said nervously.

"The envelope had no postage on it. He never mailed it."

As Joanna's face reacted to this little bombshell, Pace realized that he hadn't yet allowed the thought to fully solidify in his brain. The idea of a writer, having written something so beautiful, being sabotaged by their nearest and dearest, had been too harsh for him to dwell on the night before.

"Oh my god!" said Joanna, "How awful. Poor granny!"

"Exactly," he said.

"Pace! What are we going to do? I mean, we can't tell her. Obviously. I mean—we definitely can't tell her about the note and the envelope. She worshiped my grandfather. She'd be devastated."

"Let alone the fact that she could've had a successful writing career."

"But we don't know that."

"Oh yes we do. I read it."

"You read it?"

"Yep. The whole thing. It's not very long. I finished it not long before you had your nightmare."

"Oh my god!" she almost shouted. "My nightmare!"

"Yeah. I already thought about that. Spooky, huh?"

"Very spooky," she said, mulling things over. "So—you read it. And?"

"And—it's brilliant."

"*Really*? I guess I shouldn't be so surprised, but—I mean—well, wasn't it—very old-fashioned?"

"Not at all. It could've been written yesterday."

"Really?"

"Really."

"Well—so—um—what's it about?"

Pace drew another deep breath.

"Well, it's about a lot of things. First of all, it's called *The Best of Lives*—and there's a heading over the prologue that says *"The best of lives are made up of second choices."* Anyway, it's about this debutante who gets pregnant out of wedlock—back during the baby boom—and all hell breaks loose in her family, of course. And, the guy is being forced to marry her, of course. But then, it starts to take on this kind of feminist vibe. She decides to stay on in her family's summer house, like, way after the season, where she has an affair with her piano teacher—although, I guess it's not an affair if you're not married. Anyway, she refuses to marry the guy who the family *assumes* is the baby's father, and she kind of hides from everybody—which drives everybody nuts. In fact, they end up deciding *she* must be nuts, and even consider having her put away at one point. I mean—she does do some really bizarre things."

"Like what?"

"Well, like—she becomes obsessed with this guest room that she decides to make into a nursery. She decides that life is just too hard for girls, and she convinces herself that if she keeps putting more and more blue things into this room, somehow the baby will be a boy."

"And was it a boy?"

"Yes, she does end up having a boy—in Europe—and she ends up marrying the guy, but her family ships her off because they know the kid's gonna be born way too soon. Then they swoop in and put the kid up for adoption somewhere and she never sees him again. And then they have another baby—a girl—and then her family gives her the house as a wedding present—oh, it's in Newport, by the way—and then, she begins taking everything that's blue out of the nursery, but she still calls it the Blue Room, and—"

"Pace!" said Joanna, wide-eyed.

"I think I know what you're gonna say."

"It's about *her*! Or—at least—it *could* be."

"Holy shit."

"You can say that again."

"*Holy shit.*"

"I'm totally speechless."

"You know," said Pace, "I just realized something. Maybe that's why he didn't want it to be published."

"Of course. That makes total sense."

"Maybe he was trying to protect her."

"And himself," said Joanna. She wasn't yet ready to let her grandfather entirely off the hook. "But I can't imagine her writing a book like that—I mean, that people could see right through."

"Well—maybe she just used the whole blue room thing as a tease—or an inside joke—you know, to her friends—and made the rest of it up."

"Yeah, maybe," said Joanna. "Or maybe it's partly true. They say you should write about what you know, don't they? Or maybe she was going through temporary insanity. I think it runs in the family."

"Whatever," said Pace. "I really think we should try to get it published. I mean, if she wants to. My mother knows some people in publishing."

"Why does that not surprise me?"

"Yeah, right. Go ahead. Have your fun. But hey—speaking of my family—I should probably be heading home soon."

"Yeah. Something tells me there's going to be an explosion out there today."

They both rose simultaneously, hugged, and kissed.

"You go see about your family," said Joanna, "and I'll go check on mine."

—21—

Anthony Harris, having recently changed his stage name from Tony Darcy back to the name he'd grown up with in West Yorkshire, had been making the rounds of auditions for months, but to no avail. Now and again, an encouraging response would look promising—only to end up as a pretext for a sexual assignation. And even that tenuous connection to his profession needed to be conducted *chez lui*, because no one must ever be allowed to see Tony's flat in Islington. That is, if you could call a dilapidated bedsitter that still had an outdoor WC in 1973 a flat. He'd even gone so far as to create, or rather embellish, a flat-mate, whom he called Cyril, as an excuse for never having anyone up.

"Let's meet at the pub, shall we?" he would say to his few would-be visitors. "I'd ask you up, of course, but Cyril's in this evening," adding—when it was relevant—"and there's just the one bedroom."

In truth, however, Cyril did exist.

"Cyril, my darling!" Tony would always say as he returned to the flat. "Lovely to see you again. How was your day?" upon which Cyril—whose full name was Cyril Calico, responded with his customary "Meow."

"My day?" Tony might respond, "Oh, the usual. Bloody hellish. if you must know. *Mais c'est la vie au théâtre, n'est-ce pas?*" This was usually followed by a more pronounced "Meow" that Tony had decided was Calico for "*Mais, oui!*"

The first few times these exchanges had occurred had made him laugh; but lately it had begun to worry him. He was barely twenty-five years old, but the dreariness of his existence had begun (as he would half-jokingly tell the lads at the pub) to sap his will to live. It had been nearly six months since he'd left the repertory company, and things were not going quite as planned. Not is the least. More often than not, meetings and auditions followed a predictable pattern. His résumé, at a glance, looked impressive enough. After all, he'd played nearly every standard juvenile part one could mention.

There would be the inevitable raising of the eyebrows and pursing of the lips, and even an occasional "Well done, you." But then they would glance over to where the director's name was listed, and see the name Hugh Merriweather typed next to every credit, at which point the eyebrows would relax and the pursing of the lips would assume a more sinister aspect.

"Is he still with *her*?" the older ones would ask. The younger ones would ask "Is he still alive?" It hadn't taken Tony long to realize that these were merely bitchy rhetorical devices that neither required nor expected an answer—beyond perhaps an apologetic smile.

Tony had spent the past several years touring in Hugh Merriweather's little repertory company, playing opposite (and sleeping opposite) Merriweather himself, and having, for the most part, a grand time. Alas, the company's principal actress, Elsie Mangrove, had never been fond of young Tony. She'd once been married to Merriweather herself, back in the day when men with Hugh's sexual 'proclivities' were well advised to get married at least once.

Merriweather and Mangrove, as they were always referred to, had once made a hit on the West End. "Some Noel Coward piece, wasn't it? Or was it Rattigan?" veterans in the business would ponder aloud to Tony. "Back in the 40s, wasn't it? Or was it the 30s? Oh, well—whatever it was, it was well before my time."

After a long run in London, they had made a hit of the same play in New York. When the play finally closed, they stayed on in New York, but given that only secondary roles were being offered them, they set out for Hollywood, where English actors were then much in demand. (Secondary roles in films, after all, were another matter entirely.)

Thanks to their New York agent, they were able to arrange a few screen tests, but neither of them could quite figure how to adapt an acting style that had been honed in large, unamplified auditoriums to the necessary intimacy of a movie camera and a microphone. In an ambiguous stroke of luck, their big hit play was soon to be made into a film, with two of MGM's biggest stars playing the roles Hugh and Elsie had made such a success in. The film's director, who was known for having a rather sadistic sense of humor, thought it would be amusing to offer the second leads to the two original stage stars, and further suggested that that angle of the casting should be played up in the advance publicity.

Hence, Hugh and Elsie were both crushed and elated at the same time—but the blow was softened considerably when their agent informed them of the salaries he'd negotiated. On the downside, they could easily imagine how tongues would wag back in New York, and even more so in London, regarding the ironic ignominy of their film debut—but, on the upside, they would make more money doing one picture than they could make in an entire year of doing theatre.

Sadly, the roles of the second leads, a pair of married actors who overacted offstage as much as they did onstage, had been written for actors who were masters of the craft of drawing-room comedy, which Hugh and Elsie—who were still at the outset of their careers—were not. The reviews were scathing, the picture flopped abysmally, their option was not picked up by the studio, and when their agent no longer took their calls, the writing was on the wall.

Returning to England during the war, they discovered they'd been nearly forgotten already, and found themselves, like most everyone else, in a dwindling pool of options. It didn't help matters that everyone had seen their one Hollywood film (although all but the most unkind pretended they had not). Ever the opportunist, handsome Hugh Merriweather managed to sleep his way into a prominent position in a theatre company run by a legendary actor-manager, who died not long afterward. Being by nature an entrepreneur, Hugh wasted no time re-casting the company's productions with a marquee that read "West End stars Hugh Merriweather & Elsie Mangrove" starring in such-and-such. For a while, they even had the audacity to add "Just returned from their successful stint in Hollywood," knowing that virtually no one outside of London would be any the wiser.

And thus was born what would become a career touring perennially in rep, where, to everyone's surprise—including the *soi-disant* West End stars themselves—Hugh and Elsie actually became minor stars by building up a following who never failed to fill the houses in cities like Birmingham, or Manchester, or Liverpool, or Bristol, or Sheffield, or Leeds. Or anywhere but London.

It was while they were playing at Leeds, in 1969, that a stage-struck nineteen-year-old named Tony Harris had auditioned to join the company. Having appeared in the odd local production of Shakespeare or Gilbert and Sullivan, his résumé was—like Tony himself (as Hugh put it)—slim but meaty. Moreover, he had a certain something that transmitted itself charmingly from the stage. If that weren't enough—and it was—he was also what Hugh's generation of gay Englishmen referred to as "pale and interesting," which was code for "attractive and most likely one of us."

At the time, and given the time, Tony Harris was not convinced of his homosexuality; but in time, given the time, he found himself thoroughly involved with a handsome older man who also happened to be his employer. And, at a stage in his life when he was no more certain of his acting ability than he was of his sexuality, having Hugh Merriweather as his biggest fan was an undeniable boon. A few years later, however, Hugh's attention shifted to a newer, and more suitably mature, member of the company—the only upside of which was that Elsie suddenly found young Tony to be possessed of unsuspected charms—so much so that she even encouraged him to strike out on his own.

"You're much too young and good-looking—and *much too talented*" she said, "to going on playing in rep indefinitely."

It was just the boost he needed; or so he thought. He didn't yet realize that the security that was offered by the little troupe, both financially and emotionally, had been vital to his existence. Furthermore, he hadn't stopped to consider the fact that his reviews, while always positive, had never exactly been effusive.

And now, here he was—living in a seedy London boarding house on what little he'd saved, along with a modest weekly stipend from his mother. He knew that she could easily afford more, but she was sending an amount that would have provided for him very nicely if he were still living in Leeds—

and he could never bring himself to tell her that it barely covered his rent, meagre as it was, in London.

One dreary evening, while mulling over the day's events with Cyril, he noticed that one of the letters which had just arrived was from Hugh Merriweather.

"What do you suppose *he* wants," he asked Cyril, who meowed back on cue.

The letter, written in Hugh's typically effusive style, was the very fillip Tony was desperately in need of.

"Cyril!" he shouted, causing Cyril to jump off his lap and run about six feet away, thus arriving on the other side of the flat.

"Cyril! It's an offer!" he shouted again, as poor Cyril cowered in a corner and meowed back timidly.

The offer—to play the role of Algernon in *The Importance of Being Earnest*—was not only a wonderful artistic challenge, but Hugh was also offering him twice his former weekly salary. And as if that weren't enough, the performances would be at a charming little theatre he knew very well near Windsor Castle. It wasn't London, but it was near enough to London that, as Hugh stressed in his letter, there was no telling who might turn up.

Of course, Hugh being Hugh, the letter was also filled with company gossip, the salient bit of which was that Elsie had refused the part of Lady Bracknell—whereupon she decided she was long overdue for a holiday, adding that she planned to take her son Terrence (who'd been scheduled to play Algernon) along with her.

"I know," wrote Hugh, *"that you're asking yourself how such a ham as she could refuse a part that would allow her to chew up all the scenery south the Midlands, but she insists (I hope you're sitting) that she's far too young to play the part. I told her that, just because every senile hag with one foot in the grave plays Lady Bracknell (conveniently overlooking the fact that her daughter is a barely legal debutante), that it might* <u>*just*</u> *be an innovation, for once, to imagine that Lady Bracknell had not given birth to*

Gwendolen in the dower house. Never mind (I added rather cruelly), that your precious Terrence will soon be able to play Lear with no questions asked. (Not remotely true, of course, but I was angry with her.)

"The problem—dearest Tony—is that she got a recent notice in Bristol which began 'Elsie Mangrove remains a most handsome woman. However—'

"Terrence insists she never got past the word 'however,' although I'd be very much surprised if she got past the word 'remains.' (Our newest ingénue says she hopes Terrence enjoys skiing, as she's certain that Elsie's 'holiday' will be spent under a surgeon's knife in Switzerland.)

"In any case—dearest, dearest Tony—unless you're otherwise engaged, do please rescue us from the breach. It's a charming little production (It ought to be—it's costing me the earth!) and I know you'll be perfectly thrilling in the part."

As ever,

Hugh

As Tony read the letter, he was laughing, but also fighting back tears. He'd forgotten how amusing Hugh could be, and he hadn't fully realized how much he missed, not only acting, but also Hugh and the entire company, including Elsie.

It was time to celebrate.

"D'you know what, Cyril?" he shouted. His voice was not as fortissimo as before, but even so, Cyril's response was timid enough to cause Tony to move toward him and gently stroke his fur.

"Poor darling," he said, leaning over to give Cyril a kiss, "You must feel as if you're living with Bette Davis. Well, don't you worry, my pet. Dad-dee's going to feed you now—and no rats—although you'd probably like that—and then he's off to the pub."

—22—

Rehearsals for the "Newport premiere" of *The Importance of Being Earnest* began in mid-September, shortly after what would have been Louisa's sixty-eighth wedding anniversary. Seth Livingston had been gone for over a decade, but Louisa still observed the date in some special way—usually going over old photo albums—as she and Seth had often done on their anniversaries when they were still together. This year, for whatever reason, she missed him more than ever. The play, she thought, couldn't have come at a better time. She needed a project—and a prospect—and this one seemed perfectly suited to her needs.

The role of Lady Bracknell, while pivotal (and certainly meaty) is not particularly large—and it is therefore not uncommon for actresses in their seventies and eighties to take on the part. All of that notwithstanding, Louisa had considerable difficulty learning her lines. Joanna had started running her lines with her in the week prior to rehearsals and, when she could remember them correctly, her delivery was always funny enough to make Joanna laugh—which Louisa saw as a portent of success. Nevertheless, when she flubbed a line, she reminded Joanna that she'd never acted in her life.

"Don't worry about it," Joanna would say, adding things like "Nobody will be able to tell," or, "It's the perfect role for your stage debut."

To a great extent, Joanna was right in this. Due to the sui generis style in which the role was written, and the manner in which Louisa spoke and comported herself, there was no reason to fear that she wouldn't be able to pull it off, especially when surrounded by other amateurs. She'd somehow conveniently forgotten about Harris's past, and it didn't occur to her that the other amateurs might have professional backgrounds—or at least a good deal more experience in community theatre. Still, as the day approached, she found herself becoming somewhat nervous—which was not, as she reminded herself too often, conducive to memorizing her lines.

Alas, the first scene to be rehearsed on the first day of rehearsal was the famous scene in which Lady Bracknell interviews Mr. Worthing. It was something of a blessing for Louisa that Harris was not called to rehearse that day, although she *might* have preferred to have him present, if only for moral support. Sure enough, she flubbed a critical line here and there, but the others present, including the director, laughed heartily at her delivery of the lines—particularly those about the handbag. Despite her innate gravitas and sense of decorum, Louisa surprised herself by turning out to be something of an innate actress—at least insofar as Lady Bracknell was concerned. Fortunately for her, it's Lady Bracknell's gravitas and sense of decorum that makes the character funny.

Little by little, as rehearsals continued and Louisa felt a new lease on life, she began to say most of her lines correctly and—when the performances began—she discovered that, in the rare instances when she "went up" on a line, she could improvise something that was near enough to the original, and almost as funny. Joanna was relieved, but also happy, mainly because she had read somewhere about the benefits which might accrue to an elderly person when they assume new interests, particularly when it involves working the parts of the brain concerned with memory. For his part, Anthony Harris, as he was billed, turned in a performance that delighted Louisa, while pretty much astonishing Joanna and Pace.

Louisa had hired a caterer to arrange an opening night party at Windstone for the cast and crew and a few friends. A few tables and chairs were set up in the ballroom and, as Louisa put it, everyone had a "jolly good time." One of the cast members, Helen Thomas, the administrator of Joanna's rehab, who played opposite Harris in the role of Miss Prism, was beside herself at being a guest of Louisa Winthrop Livingston. Harris, on the other hand, while grappling with the unfamiliar experience of being a guest at Windstone, was equally ill-at-ease about being called Tony, or even "Tony darling" by his cast-mates in front of Louisa, Joanna, and Pace—whereas, for her part, Louisa accepted compliments on her performance as though she were the Empress of Persia receiving tribute from foreign ambassadors.

"That's very kind of you to say," she would say, in the grand manner, to each fan who stopped by her table. Joanna and Pace were trying not to laugh at her, but they nearly lost it when she told one of her admirers (while gesturing toward Harris, as though he was her professional confederate), "Well, you know how it is, darling. We do what we can." They knew that they should find her grandiosity a little ridiculous, but it was too wonderful to see her enjoying herself so much.

The only person at the head table who wasn't enjoying himself in quite as carefree a manner as the others was Pace. His family situation of late was becoming grim. His father was barely speaking to him at present, feeling that he may have unnecessarily implicated his brother in what was now becoming a serious legal entanglement for Clay. In addition to that, Pamela, William, and even Derek had attended the performance, and were now seated together at the next table. Pamela had greeted Pace very warmly, but he was convinced that he had noticed an uncomfortable look or two coming from her—which he could well understand. Unbeknownst to him, Joanna had made it clear to Pamela that, while she fully understood the awkwardness of the situation, she didn't want to lose Pamela as a friend—and yet, she had no intention of seeing any less of Pace either.

—23—

Once all the fun and the stress of the early autumn was past, everyone more or less retreated to their corners. Pamela was busier than ever with her work—as well as being embroiled in her litigation against Clay Hamilton. Bearing in mind Abraham Lincoln's admonishment that a lawyer representing themselves has a fool for a client, Pamela had quickly found a male attorney who'd been recommended by a colleague, only to discover that they were attracted to one another—which resulted in Pamela reverting to her original instinct to find a woman attorney—as well as resulting in some very pleasant dates with the male attorney. During all that, Pace and his mother, as well as Joanna and Louisa, had the welcome distraction of the documentary film to think about—while Louisa, again with help from Caroline Hamilton, prepared her memoirs for publication—a joyous task, when it wasn't bittersweet.

In the meantime, Harris literally retreated to his corner, which is to say: the secluded corner of the butler's pantry that was his favorite place on earth. Louisa had recently added more staff to Windstone. There was now a full-time gardener, two new full-time maids, and a new cook, a delightful Quebecois by the name of Marcel Lamotte.

Monsieur Lamotte, as it turned out, added spice to Windstone in more than the obvious way. Marcel's partner of thirty years had recently passed away, which had prompted him to seek new surroundings and new horizons. Harris, on the other hand, had been single for decades—and, although he was now sixty-eight, and Marcel a mere fifty-eight—once that glacier started to melt, they weren't going to let something as trifling as a decade stand in their way.

Occasionally, and more so as the winter holidays approached, Louisa would have an old friend or two over for tea. There was so much to talk about now: she'd decided to relegate her novel to the mists of time, but she was excited about being in the home stretch with regard to her memoirs. Then there was her lovely, talented granddaughter (and, of course, her recent life upon the wicked stage) to talk about. Joanna became so optimistic about her grandmother's comeback as a hostess that she suggested to Louisa that she should throw a costume party for Halloween.

"Precious one," said Louisa, with playful condescension, "I don't throw costume parties. I give masked balls." As soon as the words had left her mouth, however, she laughed at how ridiculous she sounded. "Good Lord!" she said. "I just sounded like a combination of Perle Mesta and Madame de Pompadour."

"Well, at least you didn't say *bals masqués*."

"Again—*very* impressed that you knew that."

"You have three books in the library about Madame de Pompadour," said Joanna. "Don't you think that fact alone might inspire me to read at least *one* of them?"

When Thanksgiving arrived, Marcel—with a little help from Harris—outdid himself; and the formal dining room became the scene of a sumptuous buffet. Louisa insisted on a buffet in order that Harris and Marcel could join the company—which included Joanna and Pace, as well as Pamela and her attorney boyfriend, Erik. The Hamiltons traditionally migrated to Palm Beach from just before Thanksgiving to just after New Year's Day, but Pace had decided to stay in Newport for Thanksgiving. Also present were one of Louisa's oldest friends—indeed, one of her bridesmaids—Millicent Sloane-Sutherland, along with Jon Harland, the artistic director of the local theatre company, and his best friend and muse, Helen Thomas.

The meal was, in Millie Sloane-Sutherland's words, "simply divine." Millicent, Lady Sutherland, had lived, for the most part, in England for several decades, where she was married to a stuffed shirt by the name of Sir Michael Sutherland—and hence, she found the guest list and the dining arrangements rather unorthodox—but no less amusing for all that.

Pace had now begun spending most nights at Windstone. When Joanna had first asked Louisa if he might stay over for a night, Louisa had consented enthusiastically—on the condition that the two of them shared the Blue Room—because she didn't want to hear people "scuttling about in the hallway all night." Indeed, he had become a part of what Lady Sutherland might call the unorthodox but happy little family at Windstone. As Christmas approached, however, Pace felt that his presence would be more or less required in Palm Beach, and he reluctantly took his leave of his new extended family.

More or less at the same moment, Joanna and Louisa had the idea of "having Christmas early," in order that Pace might join the festivities before his departure. Also, almost at the same time, they decided to ask Harris and Marcel, who had no other family, to join them. As she apprised Harris of the holiday plans, there was something in the way Louisa said, "I do hope you and Marcel can join us as you did at Thanksgiving" that made him realize that, of course, everyone knew.

And so—as they all gathered around the Christmas tree in the library or sang carols at the piano in the ballroom—a good time was again had by all.

—24—

Rehearsals for *Earnest*, (the theatrical shorthand of the cognoscenti) began two weeks later in, of all places, London. The company had played the outskirts before, but this time Hugh had actually sprung for a studio *in town*—which lifted everyone's spirits. Rehearsing the play anywhere, of course, could lift the spirits of a zombie, but no one's spirits were riding higher than those of Tony Harris. He didn't even mind the crunch of the rush-hour tube trains, with all the condescending looks from the men in their Savile Row suits, as he tried to avoid rubbing against them in his Carnaby Street castoffs.

Given that Elsie had taken Terrence and gone on holiday (they were, in fact, no further away than Slough), the company's standby grande dame, Brenda Thicke, had decided to delay her planned retirement. Brenda's husband, Basil Thorndike, had suggested that playing Lady Bracknell—in London, as it were—would be a far more fitting swan song than her most recent, very well-received performance of Alice in *Henry V*. This meant that Basil's swan song would be Reverend Chasubon, but that was entirely suitable for him, as it required no more than the modest amount of energy he was still able to muster.

On the first day of rehearsal, Brenda was the first to greet Tony—with semaphore gestures—as though he were the Prodigal Son; followed, in an effusive but more retrained fashion, by Basil and the rest of the company. Hugh himself, who was "only directing this time," waited for the general outpouring to subside, after which, as if on cue, the company parted like the Red Sea in order to allow Hugh and Tony a clear path for their big moment.

"*Darling*," said Hugh, in his best Restoration comedy manner. "How we have *all* missed you." After which he hugged Tony as though for all time and added, "Such fun it's going to be!"

Tony—shy as ever except when onstage—merely smiled and blushed, thanked everyone, and said "Lovely to see you all."

Once the greetings and the pleasantries had subsided, Hugh rang a little bell—a superstitious habit of his which everyone knew marked the official start of a new production—which meant a read-through of the entire play.

"Ah—the dinner gong!" said Brenda, as she always did, taking her seat at the table with the rather ostentatious aid of an apprentice.

"There are no footmen in this play," said Hugh to the apprentice, who then scurried to his appropriate seat—following which Hugh glanced ominously around the room to make sure all eyes were fixed on him, after which he smiled and said, "In your own time."

The read-through, as is always the case with read-throughs, was punctuated by more laughs than could ever be expected in an actual performance—accompanied by a torrent of apologies for every little misstep. Besides having seen at least ten productions of the play, Brenda Thicke could well remember, twenty years earlier, having seen the film version a minimum of ten times—and was unable to dislodge the inimitable voice of Dame Edith Evans from her mind—and was thus unable to avoid doing a blatantly transparent imitation of the immortal Dame's crowning achievement. Over and over she would say, "Oh, we'll have to fix that, won't we?" to which everyone responded, with blatantly transparent insincerity, such things as "Not at all, darling. Not. At. All."

At one point, Basil reached for his wife's hand and said, "You mustn't change a thing, my dear. Not one jot or one tittle," at which point Hugh began scribbling his notes even more feverishly—and conspicuously—than he had previously done.

After that, rehearsals went on as they usually did, although everyone began to notice that, after a few days, Hugh seemed uncharacteristically pleased with absolutely everything. Even when the sort of major cockups that normally drove him to distraction occurred, he simply smiled and said, "Let's have another go, shall we?" As everyone in the company knew all too well, a few weeks earlier, Hugh and Elsie had been summoned to London as last-minute replacements in a benefit, where they had filled in for a famous couple who were to read some of the letters of Robert and Elizabeth Barrett Browning. What everyone in the company did *not* know was that Hugh and Elsie had made three other brief trips to London in the intervening weeks, and had just been offered the leads in a television comedy series that would make them both, over the coming years, household names throughout the United Kingdom.

The series, as Tony Harris was to discover only many years later, could not have been more ideally suited to his former mentor and his sometime nemesis. It was to be called *Upstaged*, and Elsie would be playing a former stage actress who'd married an aristocrat who was recently deceased, while Hugh would be playing a former lover and colleague of hers who'd fallen on hard times, and who was now her recalcitrant and very outspoken butler. Therefore, after decades of struggle and dues-paying, Hugh Merriweather surmised, correctly as it turned out, that his ship had finally come in.

This marvelous news made for a rehearsal period that Basil Thorndike said was "the happiest I can recall," but one which he and Brenda, among others, should have known can also be the kiss of death. It is more or less an axiom in the theatre that when the cast has a wonderful, carefree time of it during rehearsals—the audience ultimately does not. As a result, the production, while not unsuccessful commercially, left something to be desired. There was a stilted quality to it, as one critic observed, that appeared to be the result of relying too heavily on the indomitability of the material—a pitfall, he further observed, to which the play in question was especially susceptible.

Notwithstanding all that, a good time was had by almost all, and no one enjoyed the experience quite as much as Tony Harris—who now dreaded, with every fiber of his being, the prospect of returning to his recent existence in Islington. Apropos, and with considerable trepidation, he approached

Hugh at a company party he'd arranged after the closing night's performance.

It was with some difficulty that he managed to get Hugh alone, and matters were further complicated by the knowledge that he knew he should wait until his bibulous former employer had imbibed a sufficient amount of alcohol to be reasonably pliable. The difficulty there, however, was that it was in that very state when Hugh was most inclined to become the life and soul of the party. Furthermore, to everyone's astonishment, Elsie Mangrove had attended the performance—and the party to boot—where she lavished compliments on one and all to a suspiciously fulsome degree. Her date for the evening was said to be a television producer of some consequence, which everyone assumed to be the main reason for her effusive outbursts.

The television producer, as it happened, had also brought two very grand looking ladies in tow. They had both been guests of the queen at a Windsor Castle entertainment known as a dine-and-sleep the previous evening, and had stayed on in a local hotel in order to see the play. After Tony had managed to take Hugh aside long enough to inquire whether there might be something for him in the company, Hugh informed him (and he mustn't breathe a word of this to anyone as yet), that he would soon be disbanding the company. Not long after that, a dejected Tony found himself making the acquaintance of the two grand ladies—who turned out to be American—not that anyone would ever have guessed it from the manner in which they spoke.

"Millie S-S," as her friend "Rose" Livingston called her, had also had a cocktail or two more than she should have, and, as a result, ambled up to Tony Harris, along with her friend.

"Young man," she said, "I am Lady Sutherland, as you are no doubt aware—and this is my oldest friend in the world, Mrs. Seth Livingston of New York and Palm Beach."

"How do you do," said Louisa Livingston to the young actor. "I thought you were splendid in the play."

"That's very kind of you, ma'am," he said. "I enjoy the part very much."

“Yes, yes,” interrupted Millie, “that’s as may be—but my friend here—Mrs. Seth Livingston—has come all the way from New York to London with the express purpose of finding herself an English butler, and I told her I think you’d be a pip. Merriweather tells us your parents were in service in Yorkshire.”

“Millie—stop,” said Louisa, attempting to smile through her embarrassment. “This young man is an actor, and a good one.”

“I’ll take it!” said Tony, as much to his own surprise as to that of the two women. “I’ll take the job! I’ll do it!”

“But,” said Louisa, “well—what about your career?”

“I don’t have a career, ma’am,” he said. “Nor I do anticipate having a career—and I’m not at all sure that I want a career.”

“Oh, yes,” said Louisa to Millie, “He’ll do very nicely.” Then, smiling at young Tony, she said “Yes. You’ll do very nicely—and—not to sound like Gwendolen in the play, but—I’ve always been inordinately fond of the name Anthony. Although, I suppose I’ll have to call you Harris, won’t I?”

Thirty-three years later, a few months after the death of Seth Livingston, his beloved English butler Harris, while sorting through things in Mr. Livingston’s room, came across, among other unexpected things, what appeared to be a manuscript for a novel written by Mrs. Livingston when he himself was only two years old. His natural impulse was to request permission to read the manuscript, but he knew Mrs. Livingston well enough to know that she’d most likely say something like “Oh, that silly old thing,” after which she’d thank him for his interest and toss it into the fireplace.

Despite feeling that he was overstepping an unmarked boundary, his curiosity got the best of him, and he took the manuscript to his pantry, and later to his room, where he spent a sleepless night absorbed in the story and what he surmised to be its implications. He had already conjectured, based on an attached cover letter on the unstamped envelope, that his late employer, for whatever reason, did not wish to see the manuscript published. That apparent fact had piqued his interest almost as much as the fact of the manuscript itself. After reading the novel, however, his imagination took flight. For one thing, it was a beautifully written and engrossing story, but—even more potently than that—the details of the story rooted him more or less to the spot.

He had been told, while still a small child, that he had been adopted, and that his surname had been changed to conform with that of his adopted family in Yorkshire. He also knew, from his years of employment by the Livingston family, that not long after the Winthrop-Livingston wedding, the former Millicent Sloane had married a fabulously rich English industrialist—a titan of industry who was just the sort of man to whom everyone in government was likely to owe favors. The twists and turns in Mrs. Livingston's novel had sparked Harris's imagination sufficiently to make him wonder: what if—as was the case with the infant in the story—*he* was the result of an extra-marital affair on the part of the young Mrs. Livingston? And if that were the case, to whom would Mrs. Livingston have been more likely to turn for assistance than the newly wed and newly powerful Lady Sutherland? It seemed abundantly clear that, for whatever reason, Mr. Livingston had suppressed the book from publication. Surely the story wasn't a *roman à clef* account of the Livingstons themselves—but was it perhaps a little too close to home to be published? There had even been a couple of occasions when a family friend had said that Harris bore something of a resemblance to Louisa.

"He should," Louisa would say in a pointed way, "After all, he's one of the family."

Was this meant merely as a compliment? Or was it more than just a compliment? If so, that would mean Mrs. Livingston was aware of having her illegitimate son as her butler. Surely that couldn't be the case. Or—did Lady Sutherland know (or suspect) the connection and not share it with her lifelong friend? From what little Harris had seen of her on her infrequent visits, she could be quite superficial and self-involved. But could she be *that* self-involved? One thing was certain: there could be no question of a butler broaching such a subject with his employer—ever.

The next day, for the first time within anyone's memory, Harris moved through his duties with something less than his customarily unswerving efficiency. At times, he seemed almost sluggish. When he had assured Mrs. Livingston, based on her inquiry, that he was feeling perfectly well, she remembered that he had spent a good portion of the previous day in her late husband's room—and she therefore took Harris's ruffled demeanor as a token of his respect for his late employer—and she was deeply touched by it.

EPILOGUE

On a beautiful late spring morning, almost two years after her arrival at Windstone, Joanna sat at the bottom of the lawn inhaling the sea breeze coming off the Atlantic. She had recently celebrated being "clean and dry" for two years—and there was no doubt in her mind that it was the best thing she'd ever done for herself. So much had happened in the past two years—some of it sad, but almost all of it good. To begin with, she'd discovered a family she had never known. Two families, really. First there was her grandmother—and now there was her adopted family.

The documentary had been a pleasure for everyone involved, and there had been a screening at a local cinema, followed by a party at Hamilton Court. The wounds in the Hamilton family seemed to be healing—partly because Caroline had finally threatened to leave her husband if he didn't make the effort required. Clay had managed to escape the kind of harsh punishment that would have been administered to a less privileged culprit—although he did submit to a range of treatments with at least outward sincerity.

Louisa's memoirs had been hastened into print to allow her the opportunity to do a few bookstore signings and interviews before her waning energy began to give out. During a signing and talkback event for the book, someone in the audience had asked Joanna, who was seated on the dais near Louisa, if there was a favorite anecdote her grandmother had told her that didn't end up in the book. Without hesitation, she said, "I think maybe the one about Grace Kelly," after which she turned to Louisa to fill in the blanks.

"*Well,*" said Louisa into the microphone, "During the late fifties, a famous banker friend of my husband's came to stay with us in Newport for a weekend—along with some chorus girl he was dating. He asked me if I would mind putting them in our best guest room—the Blue Room we call it—but the girl thought the room was terribly drab, and she asked if I could show her something else."

At this, there was what Louisa later called "subdued merriment" from the audience.

"So I told her that, not long before she married the Prince of Monaco, Grace Kelly had once slept in that room. *Well*—that was all the inducement that was needed. Suddenly, she was in love with the room."

More subdued merriment.

"The fact is," Louisa went on, "Grace *had* stayed with us a few years earlier, but not in the Blue Room. In any case—a few years later on, the chorus girl—who'd since become a big Broadway star—was at a charity ball in Monte Carlo, where my friend Lady Sutherland introduced her to Princess Grace. As an icebreaker, she told Grace that they'd both slept in the same room at Windstone—'the famous Blue Room,' she said."

"'Oh, no,' said Grace, 'I didn't get to sleep in the Blue Room. Audrey Hepburn was in there,' after which she excused herself in order to attend to her other guests. But a moment later, she came back and said, 'You know, come to think of it, it might have been Elizabeth Taylor.'"

Here, the subdued merriment went up a notch—but it was nothing compared to what Louisa had become used to.

"You see?" she said, with a wink and a nod to Joanna, "that's why I left it out of the book."

Now, the audience laughed heartily, the way audiences do when they're brought into an inside joke.

"As a matter of fact," said Louisa, "the better story—at least for me, is that my lovely granddaughter now lives in that room, and she makes me happier than all the guests who ever stayed in there put together."

Here, there was a general "Awww," accompanied by applause, which formed a perfect wrap-up for the evening.

* * *

That was Louisa's last book event. During the recent winter, she had had a stroke that took her from her new family—the only consolation being that she passed quietly, in her sleep, with no evidence of discomfort.

Over the next few months, as the sadness of Louisa's passing began to be bearable—for everyone except Harris—the reading of her will brought the necessity for discussions and decisions. As expected, Louisa had left Joanna and Harris, as equal beneficiaries, a considerable sum of money, along with Windstone.

When they found themselves able to discuss it, they reluctantly agreed to put the house up for sale. Even after the enormous capital gains tax that was likely to be due after the sale of Windstone, the remaining sum, with or without the cash they had inherited, meant that neither Joanna—and certainly not Harris, given his age—were likely to worry about money in the foreseeable future.

Pamela and Erik had been married in a small ceremony in the ballroom at Windstone during the previous autumn. And, inspired by that ceremony, though mostly for practical reasons (and without telling anyone), Tony Harris and Marcel Lamotte tied the knot soon afterward.

When spring arrived, and Harris began to show the first signs of recovering from Louisa's death, Marcel induced him to binge-watch *Downton Abbey*, after which he managed to persuade Tony to start writing a book of his own. It was to be called *In Service*, and it was a reminiscence about his parents' years of service in Yorkshire, as well as his own decades of service for the Livingstons. There were many stories—indeed the most interesting stories of the family and their famous friends—which he would not include in the book. He was not interested in writing a book that would make money. He was interested in writing a book that would serve as a testament to, and a remembrance of, the people he had loved and admired.

Shortly before Louisa's passing, Joanna realized she was pregnant—and today was the day of her wedding—but the absence of the woman who had come to mean so much to all of them cast a bittersweet atmosphere over the proceedings. Sitting alone on the edge of the Cliff Walk, Joanna began to talk to her grandmother.

She told Louisa how much she was loved and how much she was missed by everyone—especially on this day, a day which would have made her so happy. It was some comfort to Joanna to know that Louisa had at least had the satisfaction of knowing that the wedding was forthcoming—but, oh, how she would have cried at the sight of Harris walking Joanna down the aisle. She told her that her first child would be a daughter, and that she and Pace had decided to name her Louisa Rose. She told her that they had also decided to donate all the money they would accrue from the sale of Windstone to build schools for girls, one of which was already being planned in Nigeria—and that she would use her inheritance to start an all-scholarship music school for underprivileged inner-city children in New York City, where she and Pace were planning to live.

And—speaking of music, she said—there was one thing she had lied to her about that she wanted to set straight. It was about that ill-fated first concert of hers. The truth was that Joanna had actually won a prestigious international piano competition, the outcome of which included, among other things, a concert at Carnegie Hall. The concert had been so well received that Joanna's career seemed assured. And it was after that event when she realized that it would never be the life for her. She knew that she would have to spend her entire life traveling, and that she had no gypsy spirit in her at all. She longed for a settled, secure existence—and she was fairly certain that she wanted children as well.

She could almost hear Louisa's voice responding, "Be careful what you wish for, my dear," after which she'd surely give Joanna a big hug and tell her that she couldn't be happier for her.

A little later, when she had put on her wedding dress, she walked down the grand staircase of Windstone, feeling like a princess. It was not a feeling she'd ever sought after, but one which she enjoyed nonetheless—for the moment. Marcel,

Harris and William were all waiting for her downstairs at the open door, and they all burst into applause at the sight of her. William moved to the waiting limo, where he opened the door, tipped his hat, and said "Shuttle to Hamilton Court, ma'am?"

"Sure," said Joanna, instantly feeling it was an unworthy response, as she and Harris climbed into the back seat, while Marcel set off in another car to oversee the day's culinary arrangements.

Before walking out the door, though, she had stopped to look at the copy of Louisa's memoirs that had been left there since the day of her last book-signing. She blew a kiss upwards, after which she rubbed her slightly bulging stomach, and then touched the book and repeated its title:

"Better Late Than Never," she said. "Right, Granny?"

ABOUT THE AUTHOR

Mike Mitchell is a native St. Louisan who has spent most of his adult life in New York City and Newport, Rhode Island. His first novel, ***WINDSTONE***, is an adaptation of his recent screenplay *Better Late Than Never* (Originally entitled *In The Blue Room*).

Primarily known for having had an exceptionally diverse career in the performing arts—he has performed in major venues across the United States, including the Metropolitan Opera House and the New York State Theatre at Lincoln Center, Carnegie Hall, the music Center in Los Angeles, as well as on PBS and on Broadway. In recent years, he has become known as one of the country's foremost teachers of vocal technique, both in his private studio in New York City, and for one of the nation's top universities.

His books ***THE SINGER'S SURVIVAL GUIDE*** and ***ALL-STAR CAST*: *The Autobiography of an Unknown*** will be available in the Spring and Autumn of 2018.

61788809R00111

Made in the USA
Middletown, DE
14 January 2018